The car stopped. Baby k

'Hey!' shouted Johnny,
are you goin'? Don't you

'No, thank you,' she called over her shoulder. 'I'd rather walk.'

'You're nuts. You can't walk all the way back from here in this heat.' The car door opened and slammed closed. He got into step beside her. 'For once in your life don't be so freakin' stubborn. Where are you going all by yourself up here?'

When she didn't see or talk to him, she thought about him. When she did see and talk to him, she always wound up shouting. 'Look, I told you,' she said angrily. 'I'm taking a walk. Why don't you just get back in the car and leave me alone?'

'Does your father know you're up here on your own?'

She wanted to hit him.

Also available and published by Bantam Books:

Baby, It's You
Hello, Stranger
Save The Last Dance For Me
Breaking Up Is Hard To Do
Stand By Me

Our Day Will Come

DEBBIE LEWIS

OUR DAY WILL COME
A BANTAM BOOK 0 553 40123 8
Originally published in Great Britain by Bantam Books

PRINTING HISTORY
Bantam edition published 1990

This book is set in 11 on 11¾ Palatino by
Photoprint, Torquay, Devon

Bantam Books are published by Transworld Publishers Ltd., 61–63 Uxbridge Road, Ealing, London W5 5SA, in Australia by Transworld Publishers (Australia) Pty. Ltd., 15–23 Helles Avenue, Moorebank, NSW 2170, and in New Zealand by Transworld Publishers (N.Z.) Ltd., Cnr. Moselle and Waipareira Avenues, Henderson, Auckland.

Made and printed in Great Britain by
Cox & Wyman Ltd., Reading, Berks.

OUR DAY WILL COME

One

It was a warm, clear summer night in the Catskills. The air was filled with music. The patio was aglow with colored lights. The sky was lit by a bright yellow moon and a billion shimmering stars. And beneath those colored lights and those stars and that fat, grinning moon danced Kellerman's contented guests.

Max Kellerman gazed up at the sky as though he had put it there himself. 'Am I a genius, or am I a genius?' he asked Norman as the smiling couples swirled by them. Norman looked up too. 'Dance beneath the stars at Kellerman's!' Max said with a happy sigh.

Norman, unsure of whether Max was talking to him or to the man in the moon, sighed too.

Max shook his head. 'I'm a genius, that's all there is to it.' He waved one hand towards the dancers. 'You know, I think this is the best idea I had since I invited that young singer up here, what was his name . . . Flame, Danny Flame. Folk music one minute, moonlight dancing—'

'Flare,' interrupted Norman, finally deciding that Max must be talking to him.

Max's gaze returned to earth. 'What?'

'Flare,' repeated Norman. 'Danny's name is Flare, not Flame. And anyway, I thought that having him up here was Sweets' idea.'

'For Pete's sake, Norman,' snapped Max, 'Flame, Flare, who cares what his name is? I'm trying to teach you something important here.'

Norman looked over at Max. 'You are?'

'Yes, Norman, I am. I am trying to explain to you the secret of my success.'

Norman's eyes moved across the patio to where the band was playing beneath a string of Chinese lanterns. 'You mean Sweets?'

Max slapped his forehead in exasperation. 'No, Norm, I do not mean Sweets. He's a great musician, I'm not saying he isn't. And he is an important part of Kellerman's, I would never deny that. But what I'm talking about here is flexibility. What I mean is moving with the times. What I mean is giving people what they want, even before they know they want it.' Once more he gestured to the fox-trotting vacationers. 'What I mean is taking people out of the ballroom once in a while and letting them dance beneath the stars.'

'Oh, right,' said Norman, 'sure,' wondering how Max thought this information was going to help him. 'Well, everyone does seem to be having a good time.'

Max smiled. 'Of course they are.' He looked around. Everyone *was* having a good time. There was magic in the moonlight, that's what Max always said. There were the Zimmermans, who only that afternoon had been raising their golf clubs at one another, dancing cheek to cheek. There were Benjy and Ellie Wattle, a couple who usually only spoke to one another if one of them wanted the salt passed, whispering sweet nothings in each other's ear. Max smiled to himself. Yes, indeed, there was magic in the moonlight. But whose idea had it been to bring everyone out into the moonlight? 'No doubt about it,' said Max, 'I'm a genius.'

Norman glanced over at him and took a deep breath. When Max was congratulating himself about something, it was usually the best time to ask him a favor. 'Mr Kellerman?'

'What is it, Norman?'

'You're in a good mood, right?'

Max sighed. There were times when he couldn't help feeling overwhelming compassion for Norman's parents. What must it be like having Norman Bryant around twenty-four hours a day, asking one stupid question after another, every day of the year? 'Norman,' said Max, trying to be patient, 'I'm listening to wonderful music. I'm standing under a beautiful sky. I'm watching my guests have the time of their lives – thanks to me.' He pointed into the crowd, where Johnny was dancing with a smiling woman in a blue dress and matching blue hair. 'Even Johnny Castle, New Jersey's answer to James Dean, hasn't done anything to annoy me for nearly twenty-four hours. How could I not be in a good mood?'

Norman took another deep breath. 'Right. Then could I ask you a question?'

'You just asked me a question.'

'What?'

'You just asked me—' Max stopped when he saw the baffled expression on Norman's face. 'Yes, Norman, you may ask me a question.'

'Well, it's just that . . . you know next week when Jack Benny comes up?'

Max clasped his hands behind his back. He was beginning to understand how he could not be in a good mood. 'Norman, I'm begging you, don't ruin this perfect evening for me.'

'Mr Kellerman, I'm not, I just wanted to know if when Jack Benny comes up—'

Happiness is such a fragile thing, thought Max. Just when you think it's all yours something goes wrong. Johnny starts giving you a hard time. Or your favorite daughter starts giving you a hard time. Or Norman wants to try his new routine out on Jack Benny. Max shook his head. 'Don't bug me, Norman. Let me have one night when I don't have to worry about anything.'

'Yeah, but Mr Kellerman, I just want to know if—'

The trouble with Norman was that because he had so few ideas, once he got hold of one he wouldn't let it go. Max looked up at the sky. It really was a beautiful night. He was going to remain calm. 'We'll see, Norm, OK? I'm not promising anything, but we'll see.'

Norman clapped him on the shoulder. 'Oh, Mr Kellerman, thank you. Thank you. You won't regret this, I prom—'

'Norman, all I said was we'd see. Right? I'll think about it.'

The band started playing 'All I Have to Do Is Dream'.

'Yeah, sure, Mr Kellerman, I understand, we'll see,' said Norman. 'You'll think about it.' But though his hand was still on Max's shoulder, his eyes were on the moon.

Robin's eyes were on the moon, too. 'What a night. Isn't it just perfect?'

Beside her, her eyes not on the moon but on the dance floor, Baby sighed. 'Yeah, it's all right.'

'All right? What do you mean all right? I feel like I could swim in moonlight.' Robin took a deep breath. 'And just smell that air. Smell the pine trees and the wild roses and the—'

Baby wrinkled her nose. 'I smell pot roast. Pot roast and Chanel No. 5.'

Robin threw her a dirty look. 'How can you be so unromantic, Baby? Just look at this sky!'

But Baby was too busy looking at the way Penny brushed against Johnny as she danced past him with a round little man in a white dinner jacket. 'So it's got a moon and a couple of stars,' muttered Baby, as Johnny smiled that Johnny smile at Penny over his partner's shoulder. 'Big deal.'

Robin swayed to the music. 'It's a night made for love,' she whispered.

Baby folded her arms across her chest. It was obvious from the way Johnny's partner was pressing her cheek against his that she agreed with Robin. 'Well, it's wasted on me,' snapped Baby. 'Nobody's even asked me to dance except Neil "God's Gift to the Insect World" Mumford, and Mr Margolis, who must be at least fifty and only comes up to my armpit.'

But Robin wasn't interested in Neil or Mr Margolis. She hugged herself as she did a few dance steps. 'And that song. Don't you just love that song?' She sighed dreamily. 'It makes me think of Danny. Tonight I'll dream about him, I know I will.'

Baby, her eyes still focused on the other side of the patio, made a face. If Johnny and the woman with the blue hair were to dance any slower they'd have to come to a standstill.

'I'm tired of dreaming. What's dreaming ever get you?'

But Robin was not to be discouraged. 'Oh I don't know, Baby. Dreams can come true. Look at me and Danny. I dreamed about him, but I never really thought in a million years that I'd ever meet him or that he would like me back. But I did. And he did.' She turned her face to the stars. 'And even though he's not here right now, I can still dream about him. I can imagine what it'll be like when I see him again.'

The blue-haired woman was whispering something into Johnny's ear. Baby suddenly turned her back on the dancers and stared into the bushes. 'I'm really happy for you, Robin, you know that,' she said quietly, not sounding very happy at all. 'But let's face it, not all of us have someone to dream about.'

Robin looked from her cousin to the young man on the patio with the little blue lady in his arms and the mega-watt smile on his lips. 'We don't?'

'No,' came the sharp, short reply. 'We don't.'

Johnny, the colored lights shining in his eyes and Mrs Lewisohn stepping on his feet, was wishing he were dreaming. Maybe he would wake up and find that he was back in his cabin, moonlight streaming through the window and the radio playing softly beside him. He steered Mrs Lewisohn to the left and her diamond earring scratched his cheek.

Or maybe he would wake up and find that he wasn't out here, dancing to one of his favorite songs with a woman who was as sensuous as an old brick while Max Kellerman glared at him from across the terrace, waiting for him to do something wrong, but in the staff room, the Everly Brothers singing in their pure, flawless voices, his body moving with the lonely passion of the music, and in his arms . . . in his arms . . . In his arms might be anyone he cared to dream of . . . anyone at all. Johnny's eyes searched the edges of the patio, but the dance floor was so crowded that he could catch no more than a glimpse of Robin and, beside her, the back of a brown-haired head.

And then he realized that he was staring into a familiar pair of smiling dark eyes and that those eyes were winking at him knowingly. He winked back. Penny's red lips blew him a kiss. He would wake up, dancing in the staff room, and in his arms would be Penny, just like always, just as it should be. The band moved into the last few bars of the song, but in Johnny's mind he could hear Phil and Don singing, *dream, dream, dream . . . Dream, dream, dream . . .* – and all at once the floor in front of him cleared and there he was, staring into another pair of familiar eyes. But these eyes weren't smiling.

The song ended and Sweets picked up the request card that had been handed to him. Maybe it was the moonlight, or maybe it was that old Everly Brothers' tune, but he had to stare at the card for several seconds before it made any sense. He'd been miles away, dreaming a little himself. Dreaming of things he never let himself think about anymore. When Sweets heard that song, it wasn't Phil and Don he heard singing it, it was a woman he used to know, a woman who used to sit beside him on the piano bench while he played, singing along just a little off key, her head against his shoulder and her hand on his leg.

'Play that song for me,' she'd say, putting her arms around him. And he'd always know which song she meant.

He rubbed his eyes, staring at the card in his hand. But now Mr and Mrs Carl Terhune, who were celebrating their twentieth wedding anniversary, wanted him to play 'Chicago'. Sweets turned to the band. 'Chicago' was what the Terhunes wanted to hear, and so 'Chicago' it would be. A nice bouncy, happy song. Uncomplicated and unromantic – unlike love. He looked up above him for an instant, past the swinging paper lanterns to where the stars twinkled. Yeah, Sweets thought to himself, there must be something in that moonlight – and in that corny old song.

'So, how are my two favorite ladies tonight?' beamed Max, coming up to where Baby and Robin were standing. His head was bobbing back and forth and he was snapping his fingers in time to the music.

Baby barely glanced over. 'Fine,' she said.

'Hi, Uncle Max.' Robin grinned at him grimly, trying to send him a signal, a signal that would tell him that his daughter was in a bad mood.

Max, however, was feeling too pleased with himself to notice that not everyone was enjoying this perfect evening after all. He rubbed his hands together. 'So,' he said cheerfully, 'why aren't you two beautiful girls out there, dancing beneath the stars?'

'With each other?' asked Robin.

Max laughed. 'Of course not with each other. Where are all the young men?' He scanned the dance floor, looking for young men, careful not to let his eyes rest on one certain young man. 'Didn't I see Neil around, Baby?'

'It's hard not to see Neil in that pink sports coat of his,' said Baby, unable to resist a small smile.

'And with all that gunk he puts in his hair,' snickered Robin. 'There's more oil in his head than in the whole of Texas.'

For the first time that night, Baby laughed. 'We've got the only pool in the Catskills with oil slicks,' she said.

'All right, all right,' said Max, not willing to get into the Neil Mumford argument tonight. 'Maybe not Neil. But there are plenty of other fish in the sea.'

'Yeah,' giggled Robin, giving Baby a poke in the ribs, 'but who wants to dance with a fish?'

'It'd be better than dancing with Neil,' said Baby. 'At least a fish can't put his hands all over you.'

Robin found this comment hysterical. Max sighed. Why was everyone trying to ruin his good mood? First Norman, and now Baby and Robin. This conversation had all the signs of being one of those tricky women's conversations. Max knew enough about women to know that there was something going on with Baby and Robin that he probably wouldn't want to know about even if they would tell him. Which they wouldn't. Sometimes Baby was so much like her mother that it scared him.

'Uncle Max,' gasped Robin, tugging on his sleeve, 'Uncle Max, what's the difference between Neil Mumford and an octopus?'

And sometimes Robin was so much like her mother that it absolutely terrified him. Much to

Max's relief, he was saved from having to reply by Sweets.

'And that,' Sweets was saying, reading from the square of paper in his hand, 'was a special dedication for our twentieth anniversary couple, Mr and Mrs Carl Terhune, who met and fell in love in the Windy City.'

There was a polite burst of applause. 'Isn't that nice?' asked Max. 'Their twentieth anniversary.'

'Neil Mumford has more arms!' giggled Robin triumphantly.

Suddenly a large, blustery man in a maroon suit, several gold rings flashing on his fingers, jumped on stage and grabbed the microphone away from a rather startled-looking Sweets.

'Oh my God,' said Robin, the smile vanishing from her face, '*who* is that?'

'*What* is it, you mean,' muttered Baby.

'Baby, please,' hissed Max, ever defensive of his guests.

As if in answer to their question the man boomed into the mike, 'Hi there everybody, my name's Carl. Carl Terhune.'

Everybody looked at him expectantly.

'And that,' said Carl, pointing to a shy-looking woman in a pink dress, a red rose stuck jauntily behind one ear, 'that's my better half, Paulette Terhune.'

'She probably is, too,' whispered Baby.

Paulette smiled nervously at Carl.

Sweets smiled warily at Carl. 'Thank you, Mr Terhune,' said Sweets, putting his hand back on the microphone. 'I'm sure everyone here would like to join me in wishing you and your lovely wife—'

Carl wrenched the mike out of Sweets' grip. 'Wait a minute, son, wait a minute,' he growled. 'I'm not through yet.'

'Is he drunk?' whispered Robin.

'Is grass green?' Baby whispered back.

Max had this sinking feeling in his stomach that his perfect evening was about to come to an end. Nonetheless, he hated it when anyone criticized one of his guests. At the beginning of every season, Max made all his staff learn the Five Kellerman Commandments. And the first one was: The Guest Is Always Right. 'For Pete's sake, girls,' he mumbled, 'it's the man's twentieth wedding anniversary, surely he's entitled to a little drink.'

Carl swayed unsteadily. 'I just want you all to know that that song's been mine and Paulette's for more than twenty years, but I swear I've never heard it played so beautifully before.' He staggered forward, but Sweets grabbed his arm before he could actually topple from the stage. 'Don't you think so, honey?' Carl shouted at Paulette. 'Isn't that the most beautiful version of "Chicago" you've ever heard in your life?'

Paulette shook her head up and down, smiling harder than ever.

Sweets, still smiling too, made another move on the microphone. 'Well, thank you, Mr Terhune—'

Carl turned to Sweets. 'You people really do have rhythm, don't you?' he asked. 'You sure know your music, son, you really do.'

There was a sharp intake of breath on Max's left. 'Daddy!' screeched Baby. 'Did you hear what that . . . that . . . what your guest said?'

'Baby, please, I'm sure he only meant it as a compliment.'

But the smile on Sweets' face suddenly looked like it was set in cement. 'Mr Terhune,' said Sweets, 'I really think—'

But Mr Terhune was busy stuffing a fifty dollar bill into his hand. 'You just keep playing like that, OK? You just keep that wonderful music coming. Maestro!' called Carl. 'Start that sonofagun up again!'

Sweets looked from the money in his hand to the drunken man in the maroon suit who towered over him. How could he give him back his fifty bucks and get him off the stage without a scene?

But before he could think of a solution, the problem changed. Carl started singing himself, gesturing for the audience to sing along with him.

Sweets looked at the band and the band looked at him. Resigned, he moved back to the piano. Other people joined in as the band began to play. Carl sang louder. Several couples started to dance. Maybe it was going to be all right after all, thought Sweets. Carl Terhune would sing his song and then go back to his table and the night would go back to the way it had been.

Max turned to his daughter. 'There,' he smiled, 'you see?' Just behind Baby a pale, rather beautiful face floated into view. For a fraction of a second he almost thought that he recognized that face. But that, of course, was completely ridiculous. He cranked up his smile. 'Everything's fi—'

Baby looked up to find her father staring over her head at the entrance to the patio, a peculiar expression on his face. 'Daddy?' said Baby. 'Daddy? What is it?'

'Hey, Uncle Max,' said Robin. 'What's the matter? You look like you've seen a ghost.'

But Max didn't seem to hear them. He did recognize that face. That pale skin. That dark hair. Those enormous eyes that were searching through the crowd for one person and one person only.

Baby and Robin both turned to where Max was looking. There, right by the shrub that had been cut in the shape of a K, was a woman who did not belong at Kellerman's. She was definitely not a woman who played shuffle-board or tried on wigs. She was absolutely not a woman who entered mambo competitions or pie-throwing contests. It was unlikely that this woman had ever made a pot of chicken soup or scrubbed the dead insects out of the front porch light with a toothbrush in her life. This was a woman who hung out with poets and artists and musicians. This was a woman of romance and glamor and mystery. The woman both Baby and Robin would secretly like to be.

'Oh wow,' breathed Robin. 'Who is she?'

'Daddy,' nudged Baby, unable to take her eyes away, 'Daddy, do you know her?'

At that moment those enormous eyes found the person they were looking for.

Sweets looked up to find himself staring at a figure standing in the moonlight. I must be dreaming, he thought to himself. That stupid song. All these stupid stars. The figure started moving towards him – just the way it had moved towards him a million times before. The eyes met his. The piano playing stopped abruptly. If this was a dream, then he prayed to God that he never woke up.

Max, Baby and Robin followed the figure walking towards the stage with their eyes. 'That,' said Max, 'is Martine Jellico.'

Two

Sweets and Martine, several feet apart, walked slowly away from the terrace and down the path that led to the pool.

'You understand I don't have much time, right?' Sweets was saying, his eyes straight ahead. 'I've got to get back for the second set.'

Martine nodded. 'Oh sure, I remember about second sets.' She glanced over at him. 'It hasn't been that long, you know.'

He refused to meet her eyes. 'It seems like a long time to me,' he said at last, his voice coming from far away.

Martine put her hands in her pockets and looked down at the ground, where the moonshine was making patterns on the grass. Coming up here had seemed like such a good idea this afternoon, but now she was wondering if she'd been wrong. This afternoon, walking along Greenwich Avenue in tears, making a public spectacle of herself, she had imagined the moment when Sweets first saw her. He was going to rush to her side and take her in his arms. He was going to call her 'babe', just like he used to. 'Oh, babe, babe,' he was going to say, 'I've missed you so much.' After all that had happened, everything would be all right at last.

But so far nothing, of course, had gone as she'd imagined. Instead of being dumbstruck with love at the sight of her, he'd sat there looking so horrified you would have thought Frankenstein's monster had just crashed on to the patio. Instead of falling into her arms and telling her how much he'd missed her, how he'd counted every lonely minute since they'd parted, he said, 'Hello, Martine, how's tricks?' She glanced over at him again. Yes, there he was, the same Sweets she remembered. But now he seemed as far away as the moon – and twice as cold.

This is a dream, Sweets was thinking to himself as they walked along. It is definitely a dream. The only trouble was, he couldn't decide whether it was one of the best dreams he'd ever had, or one of the worst. Without turning his head, he shifted his eyes so he could just see her beside him. That hair. Those eyes. Those cheeks. Those lips. When she'd first come over to the piano and spoken his name he'd been afraid he was going to burst into tears. 'Hi, Sweets,' she'd said, with that smile she always made when she was nervous, and the room had started spinning around him. And although the Catskill mountains were renowned for their piney woods and Kellerman's was renowned for its gardens, the only thing he could smell at the moment was Martine's perfume. It was a smell a man could drown in.

They approached the pool. During the day there was no mistaking the Kellerman pool. It belonged nowhere else but at a Catskill resort. Neil Mumford's domain, dominated by the shrill sound of his lifeguard's whistle and the sight of his bronzed body with its white hat and dark glasses constantly checking everything out, the pool area was always packed and noisy. There were sunbathing beauties with their transistors, screaming children with their inflatable rafts, and middle-aged men with Noxzema on their noses who played cards and sipped cold beers while their wives stretched out on lounge chairs and read paperback novels.

But the night, Sweets could see, had transformed it. It was no longer the place where Mrs Sheldon and Mrs Rumford sat under a beach umbrella eating corned beef on rye and arguing over the Scrabble rules, but a place where lovers met in the moonlight. It was no longer the place where little Sammy Miller lost his swimming trunks while learning to dive, but a magical place, far away from the everyday. It was hard to believe that the water shimmering in the starlight was regularly cleaned and chlorinated and not a sleepy lagoon on some tropical island. He should have taken her to the bar or the ping-pong room. He should have told her to turn around and get on the next bus back to the city. He could hear her breathe.

'So,' she said brightly, 'I guess you're surprised to see me, huh?'

'Surprised?' He grinned wryly at the couple reflected in the pool. 'Yeah, I guess you could say I'm surprised. I would've thought you'd call first or somethin'.' For the first time, he turned to look at her directly. 'Let me know you were comin', so I could bake a cake.'

Martine shrugged, trying to keep her voice both steady and jokey. 'Well, you know, I was in the neighborhood, so it seemed silly not to drop in.'

'You were in the neighborhood, huh?' He sat down on one of the loungers. 'Greenwich Village must be expanding a heck of a lot.'

She sat down beside him, careful not to sit too close. 'Oh it is, it is. It's just growing by leaps and bounds. Today Macdougall Street, tomorrow Woodstock.'

Sweets stared into the water. In a matter of seconds the world had turned upside down. He'd been sitting there at the piano, minding his own business, thinking about all the Carl Terhunes he'd seen over the years and hoping this one wasn't so drunk that he ended up barfing all over the stage. In a few hours the night's entertainment would have been over and he and the other guys would have had a drink together, or started jamming, or gotten out the cards. He'd have gotten to bed late, gotten up late, wasted the afternoon. And the next night he would have been back at the piano, minding his own business. That was the way his summers went. That was the routine of his life now. Quiet, predictable, and safe. No problems. And then, without warning, the ghosts that had been flitting through the moonlight, the memories that had been running through his mind because of that silly song, had suddenly reached out and grabbed him. He'd looked up, and there she was, walking towards him with that same old smile. One ghost. One memory.

'Martine,' Sweets said at last, no trace of the emotions he was feeling in his voice, 'what are you doing here? I thought I was never going to see you again for as long as I lived.'

The silver bracelets on her wrist jangled as her fingers tapped nervously on her knee. 'Yeah, I know—'

'That's what we agreed, remember? Just a clean break . . .' For a second it looked like he might blow his cool, but he managed to go on. 'No fuss, no muss. Remember?'

'Yeah, Sweets, I do remember. But—'

'What was it you said? Something about minimum pain?'

Martine's laugh was as light as a canon ball. 'Yeah, that was me. Miss Minimum Pain of 1961.'

'So, what's this all about?' He turned to her suddenly as a new thought occurred to him. Her skin beneath his fingertips was as warm and soft as he remembered. A chill ran through him. 'You're not in some sort of trouble, are you?' He hoped she couldn't hear the trembling in his voice. 'You're not ill or . . . you're all right?'

The bracelets clinked. 'Oh, yeah, yeah, I'm all right. I'm fine, really . . .' Now she was having trouble meeting his eyes. 'It's just that I, well . . .' She took a deep breath. 'I'm getting married.'

His hand fell away from hers. 'Married?'

'Well, yeah, I think so. I think I'm getting married. At least, I could get married.' She glanced over at him, but his eyes had returned to the couple in the pool. 'He teaches at NYU. He came into the shop one day and . . . You'd really like him, you know, and he'd like you. He's very smart and funny and affectionate . . . terminally Anglo-Saxon, of course, but nobody's perfect, are they?' Now that she'd started she couldn't seem to stop for so much as a breath. Shut up, Martine, she told herself, stop yapping away like a three-year-old, but the words came tumbling out. 'And Mark that's his name, Mark, Mark says he's ready to settle down, you know? And I, well, I look in the mirror, and I'm not getting any younger, and I guess I'm ready to settle down myself, you know, do the kids and family bit . . .'

He felt like someone had dropped a ton of concrete on his head. Sweets sat motionless beside her while she talked on and on. The last word he'd heard was 'married'. After that it had become just a jumble of meaningless sounds. If he'd known when he woke up this morning how this day was going to turn out he would have definitely stayed in bed. First he would have nailed the door and windows shut and ripped the phone out of the wall, and then he would have stayed in bed. If the world and his brother had come knocking on the door he would have said, 'Sorry, I don't need this. I'm not coming out for nobody.'

'And of course the shop's doing really well now, you know, I don't have to work so hard at it anymore, it sort of takes care of itself, so, you know how it is, I've got a bit more time on my hands and I guess I could take up karate or something like that but—'

His power of speech came back all at once. 'You came all the way up here to tell me you're getting married? Why? You want me to play at the wedding or something? You couldn't just send me a note?'

Something had happened to the connection between her brain and her mouth. It had snapped, that's what had happened. She had no control over what she was saying. 'And Mark is everything a woman could want, you know. Really. He's attractive and considerate and kind and—'

'Martine, can't you hear me? Why—'

'But he's not you,' she sobbed. A single tear trickled down that lovely cheek. 'He's terrific. He really is terrific. I go over and over in my mind all the wonderful things about him and what a sensible thing it would be to marry him, but all I can think of is you.' The bracelets were beginning to sound like a steel band. 'I can't sleep, I can't eat, I—'

He wasn't going to touch her. If he touched her he might never let go. He put one tentative hand on her shoulder. 'But Martine,' he said gently, 'you were the one . . . we agreed . . .'

The tears were falling in earnest now. 'I know, I know . . .' She started fumbling in her bag for something to wipe her eyes with. He handed her the handkerchief from his pocket. 'But I thought . . . I don't know, I had this crazy idea that maybe you still loved me.'

Max was pacing back and forth along the side of the patio. Every few paces he'd look out into the dark, in the direction Sweets and Martine had gone. Every other few paces he'd look at his watch. He looked at it now. 'Where is he?' he asked. He turned to Baby and Robin. 'I mean, a break's a break, but this guy's taking a vacation.' He gestured towards the dance floor. 'I've got people out there who want to rhumba.'

'I'm sure he'll be back soon, Uncle Max,' said Robin. 'I mean, it's not like anything could happen to him out there, is it? He just went for a walk.' She giggled. 'It's not like there are bears out by the pool or killer bats or anything.'

Max's smile was thin. 'Thank you, Robin. You can't imagine what a comfort you are to me.' Killer bats were the last thing he was worried about at the moment. Killer bats he could handle. You just waved a crucifix at them or clubbed them with a shovel or whatever. Beautiful women who broke your best friend's heart years ago and suddenly turned up in the middle of the night were another matter.

'I know, Dad,' piped up Baby, 'why don't I go and see if I can find them . . . you know, tell Sweets the natives are getting restless.'

Max looked at his youngest child. So far he had been successful in refusing to give her and Robin any information about Martine Jellico, except for her name and the fact that she was an old friend of Sweets. He'd sworn blue that she hadn't been Sweets' girlfriend. 'Don't be ridiculous,' he'd said. 'I know for a fact that they were just good friends. I think they went to Julliard together or something.' He'd pretended he knew almost nothing about her. 'I think I remember Sweets saying that she lives downtown,' he'd said. The wise old man who lived in his head was telling him that the farther away from Sweets and Martine he kept Baby the better off everyone would be. One way or another she would discover the truth. And then she would try to interfere. She would decide that she could straighten everything out, like she always did – and then God knew what calamities would occur. 'You know what she's like,' the wise old man was saying to him, 'she's a nice kid, but she's got this thing about making everybody happy.' At the same time, however, another voice, one that preferred heart to wisdom, was telling him that Baby was the only person he could send. So she discovered the whole story, so what? It had all been over a long time ago. There was nothing she could do. And even if there were . . . 'Well, what's wrong with happiness?' this voice was saying. 'Let her go. You have nothing to lose.'

Max sighed. 'I don't know, Baby. I don't like to bother Sweets. I mean, I'm sure he's just gotten carried away talking over old times . . .'

Baby patted him on the arm in a motherly way. 'Look, Dad,' she said solemnly, 'I can be diplomatic, you know. I'll just go out there and tell Sweets that the band's ready to start the next set. OK? Is there some harm in that?' She was already walking away.

'And I'll go with her,' said Robin, starting to follow. 'For moral support.'

'Whoa!' Max grabbed hold of Robin's arm. 'Oh no you won't,' he smiled. 'You'll stay here and give *me* moral support. One of you out there is more than enough.'

Somehow, the hand on her shoulder had become his arms around her and her head against his chest. What a crazy idea, that he might still love her. 'The thing is,' he was saying, his voice gentle, her hair just brushing his lips, 'the thing is, Martine, that we've been all through it, backwards and forwards, a thousand times. You know as well as I do what happened last—'

'Sweets!' Baby's voice came hurtling through the night like a spaceship from another planet. 'Sweets!'

Sweets and Martine pulled apart so abruptly that they both had to laugh.

'Who's that?' whispered Martine, wiping the last few tears away and brushing at her hair with her hand.

Sweets straightened his shirt. 'That's Max's daughter, Baby.' He could only hope that the nuclear holocaust that had taken place in him during the last half hour wasn't showing on his face.

She saw them as soon as she rounded the pool house. They were sitting side by side, pretending to be studying the chlorine level of the water. It was completely obvious that whatever had been going on between them before she turned up had been stopped in a hurry. Had they been fighting, she wondered? Or had they been locked in a passionate embrace? Baby gave herself a little pat on the back. Thank God she had had the sense to call out before they came into view. Well, she would pretend that she had no idea at all that something was going on. She would act as though the most normal thing in the world was for Sweets to disappear in the middle of a performance with beautiful women in need of someone to walk with. 'Oh, there you are,' called Baby gaily. 'We were wondering where you'd got to.'

Sweets was amazed to discover that he could actually stand. 'Well, here I am.' He turned to Martine. 'Baby, I'd like you to meet an old friend of mine, Martine Jellico. Martine owns the best book store in Greenwich Village.'

Baby smiled. 'Hi, welcome to Kellerman's.' Old friend my foot, thought Baby. This woman was no old friend of Sweets. They must have been lovers. She shook Martine's hand. Probably this woman had broken Sweets' heart.

'Martine, this is Max's daughter, Frances.'

Baby laughed nervously. 'But you can call me Baby, everybody else does.' Surely that was pain she saw in Martine Jellico's eyes. Perhaps it was Sweets who had broken her heart. Baby sighed silently. Men.

'OK, Baby,' said Martine. 'But you'll have to call me Marty.' She smiled, giving Sweets a jab with her elbow. 'Everybody else does but him.'

'Look,' said Baby, feeling awkward. 'I'm sorry to bother you guys, but Mrs Schwartz is screaming for her rhumba, and—'

Sweets held up one hand. 'Say no more. I was just going back.' He looked from one woman to the other. Both of them were watching him like they were expecting him to do something amazing – walk across the pool or something. He had to get back to the safety of the band. 'But, you know, maybe you could help Martine get settled. Show her around.' He turned to Martine. 'I don't even know if you've checked in or what.'

Martine's bracelets were making a racket again. 'Well, not exactly. I sort of got out of the cab and—'

'My pleasure,' said Baby. 'I'm only too happy to help.'

Sweets' heart gave a little thump. Help. He'd forgotten about Baby's mission to help everybody. But she was smiling at him in a totally innocent way. She had no idea of what was between him and Martine. How could she? Max would never say anything. He had nothing to worry about.

'So,' said Martine as he started to turn away. 'I'll see you after the show?'

He could hear the begging in her voice, but he'd already been through more than enough for one night. He needed some time by himself. To think. Or maybe not to think. Maybe just to feel. 'Oh, geez, Martine, I'm sorry, but there's a jam over at the Sheldrake and the guys and I are sorta committed . . . you know . . .'

'Oh sure,' said Martine, trying to keep her smile intact. 'I know. I'm kind of tired anyway. We can catch up in the morning.'

Sweets nodded. 'Yeah. I'll see you in the morning.' He winked at Baby. 'And anyway, you two will have a lot to talk about. Baby's mother just moved into the Village.'

'Oh, really?' asked Martine, trying to sound as though this news excited her.

'Yeah,' said Sweets, unable to stop himself, 'she's gonna be going to NYU.'

Three

Robin, wearing pink babydoll pajamas, her hair wrapped around several beer cans, was sitting on her bed, hugging her pillow and giving Baby the attention she usually reserved for looking in the mirror or staring at pictures of her favorite movie stars. 'I don't believe this,' Robin breathed. 'I never really thought of Sweets as having things like girlfriends.'

Baby was giving her hair its nightly one hundred brushstrokes. She was on fifty-nine. 'I know,' she said, looking thoughtful. 'Me neither. It's funny, though, isn't it? I mean, Sweets is attractive, and he's got to be one of the nicest men alive . . .'

'And he's a great musician,' put in Robin. 'Even Danny was impressed by Sweets.'

Baby counted to herself, sixty-one, sixty-two. 'Maybe it's because Sweets is so, you know, cool. I mean there's never anyone up here you could really picture him with.'

'Well, that's an understatement,' giggled Robin. 'I mean, can't you just picture him playing ping-pong with Sylvia Loyola?'

Sixty-three, sixty-four. Baby grinned. 'Which one's that? The home ec. teacher who looks like a dumpling? Or the secretary who's always offering to retype the menu?'

Robin shook her head. The beer cans rattled. 'Neither. Sylvia's the red-headed nurse. The one who threw a fit because she only came second in the shuffleboard championship. You remember. She claimed the contest was rigged.'

'Oh, I know. The snobby one who's always talking about her body.'

'That's the one!' Robin put on a high, whining voice. 'I don't think you understand, my good man, I am not accustomed to putting fat into this body . . . I'm sorry, Miss, but you'll have to fit me into the croquet tournament. My body does not feel happy unless it's had several hours of exercise a day.' She put the pillow in the crook of her arm, looking at it as though it were another person. 'I'm sorry, Mr Sweets,' she said primly. 'But my body does not like to be touched by hands that play the piano unless those hands belong to Ludwig Beethoven.'

'Oh, stop it, Robin,' laughed Baby. 'Now you've made me lose count.' She threw the brush on the bed. 'Now my hair's not going to have any special lustre tomorrow.'

Robin made a face. 'That's OK. For one day, Frances Kellerman, you'll know what it's like to be me with dull, ordinary hair. Anyway, I want to hear everything Martine told you.'

Baby looked warily at her cousin. 'But it's a secret, right? I mean, I don't think she would've told me anything except she was so upset. You know, coming all the way up here to see him and then he acts like he's got something better to do tonight.'

Robin looked offended. 'You know you can trust me!' It was almost possible to believe from the expression on her face that Robin had never in her life told a secret she'd promised to keep. 'These lips are sealed,' she swore, pretending to zip up her mouth.

'Well. . .' Baby still looked unsure. After all, the Kellerman's had an old family saying: 'There are three major forms of communication: telephone, telegraph, and telling Robin'. And of the three, Max always added, telling Robin was the fastest, the cheapest, and the most reliable. 'You swear on Troy Donohue's life?'

'Baby!'

Baby looked around as though the room might be bugged. 'OK.' She crossed over to sit beside Robin. 'I don't know what Dad was going on about them going to Julliard together. Because Martine said they met at Bennington. She was teaching literature, and he was playing in this club off campus.'

'Oh, boy,' sighed Robin. Her eyes were getting wider and wider, making her look just a little like a frog – a frog with beer cans in her hair. 'I bet it was one of those smoky jazz clubs, you know. Where everybody's incredibly intense and intellectual and—'

Baby waved a hand in front of her face. 'Robin, would you like me to continue or what?'

Robin pouted. 'I was only trying to set the mood.'

'Anyway, Martine said it was love at first sight. It was like she'd always known him, but she'd just never met him before. Like maybe they'd known each other in another life.'

Robin sighed. 'Oh, how romantic . . .'

'She was sitting with some friends at a table near the stage, and she just couldn't keep her eyes off him through the entire set.'

'This is too much.' Robin fell back on the bed. 'It really is. I just *love* love.'

'Martine said she didn't think she heard even one note of what they were playing. It was as though she was in a trance. There was something about him.' Baby wrapped her arms around her knees, her own eyes taking on an almost trance-like look. 'You know, like he was the most special person she'd ever known. She just walked in and looked over and there he was – and she knew right away that no matter what happened she would never forget him.' Baby's voice became a whisper. 'The first time our eyes met . . .'

'What? I can't hear you,' Robin popped back up. 'So then what happened?

Baby shook herself out of the dream she'd begun to slip into. 'As soon as the set was over, Sweets came over to their table and asked if he could join them. Everybody was sort of looking at each other, wondering where this guy had come from and everything, but Martine just said, sure. And he pulled up a chair and sat down next to her.'

'And then?'

'Robin!' Baby gave her a playful shove. 'What do you mean "And then?" And then she spilled her drink on his lap and they never saw each other again.' She gave her a friendly shake. 'What do you think happened? And then he walked her home and they started seeing each other.'

'Wow.'

Baby's expression became serious. 'They didn't want to get involved, you know, because of all the problems, but they couldn't help themselves.'

'Oh, I know,' sighed Robin. 'It was bigger than both of them.'

'Anyway, they went together for a while, then they broke up, then they got back together, then they broke up again . . . And now there's this other guy who wants to marry her. He's a professor. Mark, his name is. And he's really nice and everything—'

'And white?' interrupted Robin.

'Yeah, and white. And Martine really likes him a lot—'

'Don't tell me,' said Robin in a hushed whisper. 'But it's Sweets she wants to marry.'

'Exactly. Only he doesn't think they can handle it.'

'It's just like *West Side Story*.' Robin began to sing the first few lines from one of the saddest songs in the show.

'Robin! This is serious. Sweets and Martine really are star-crossed lovers. Neither of them wants anybody else, but the world is making it impossible for them to be together.' She flopped back on the bed, staring up at the ceiling. 'It just isn't fair. Why shouldn't they be allowed to love each other? They're not hurting anybody. So what if there are a couple of little differences between them?'

Robin looked over at her, a new caution in her eyes. 'A couple of little differences between them? Baby, she's white and he's colored.'

'So what? Everyone should have a right to love. Do you mean if I fell in love with someone who didn't come from exactly the same background as me that I should give him up and marry somebody else who'd been barmitzvahed and went to the right college and—'

The caution was increasing. 'Are we talking Irish mechanics here or what, Baby?'

Baby rolled over on her side. 'You know perfectly well what we're talking about, Robin. We're talking about Sweets and Martine. I was just trying to get you to agree to the principle.'

'Oh, I agree with the principle all right—'

'It's just like Romeo and Juliet,' said Baby, still gazing at the ceiling.

'Baby,' said Robin, 'You're not going to meddle, are you?'

'Romeo and Juliet were meant for each other, but the stupidity of the world wanted to keep them apart. We can't let that happen to Martine and Sweets.'

'Oh, Baby, I don't know.' Robin frowned. 'Don't you remember? Romeo and Juliet died.'

Baby had lain awake for what seemed like hours, listening to Robin snoring contentedly in the next bed. Sometimes Robin's snoring sounded like the snoring of an old dog, and sometimes it sounded like a cesspool backing up. Tonight Robin was impersonating the plumbing. But Robin wasn't the reason Baby hadn't been able to sleep herself. While Robin dreamed about Danny Flare, Baby had gone over and over everything Martine had told her.

Sure, if you looked at Martine's and Sweets' situation from one angle it was really complicated. Interracial marriages were only slightly more popular with most Americans than Communists or the Bubonic Plague. There certainly weren't any interracial couples in Roslyn, Long Island. In fact, there weren't really any colored people in Roslyn, Long Island. Not unless you counted the De Quincey's maid. But if you looked at it from another angle it was incredibly simple. Sweets loved Martine. Martine loved Sweets. One and one equals two. What could be more simple than that? The problem was, how could she help them? It was a little discouraging that even Robin, her most stalwart ally, seemed hesitant. And then Baby'd realized what she needed. She needed the advice of someone a little more worldly than she was. Someone with more experience. Someone who was close to Sweets and would understand his point of view. Someone she was sure, deep in her heart, would agree with her.

Baby stood in the doorway of the staff room. She wasn't as terrified as she used to be about going in, but it still didn't hurt to be careful. Even though Penny had been pretty nice to her lately, you could never be sure with Penny. One minute she was being all friendly and sisterly, and the next she was giving you looks that could poison a horse.

Inez Foxx was singing 'Mockingbird'. There were so many people dancing that it almost seemed as though the room itself was grooving to the beat, but still she had no trouble spotting the person she was looking for. There was no mistaking the way he moved. Even from behind Johnny exuded a power and a pleasure that none of the other kids came close to matching. She leaned against the door frame, watching, forgetting for a few minutes why she had come.

'Uh oh, lover boy,' said Penny, seeing Baby across the room, staring at them with what Penny always called *that look* on her face, 'I may be wrong, I mean, there are so many people here that it's hard to tell just who is visiting who, but I think maybe you've got yourself some company.'

'Cut it out, will ya, Pen?' said Johnny good-humoredly. Nonetheless, he turned immediately in the direction of her look.

Penny stopped dancing, watching Johnny with a funny smile on her face. 'Oh, did I make a mistake?' she asked innocently. 'Is she here for Cookie, maybe? Or Charley? It does seem a little late for a dance lesson—'

But Johnny, of course, wasn't listening to her. He was patting her on the shoulder and saying, 'Uh, Penny, look, something must've happened. I'll be right back, OK?'

'Oh sure,' said Penny, talking to him even though he was already squeezing his way through the crowd and couldn't have heard her, even if he'd been listening. 'Don't mind me. You go off and help Miss Peace Corps free Southeast Asia. I'll just stay here and dance by myself.'

Johnny sat on the porch steps, completely silent, while Baby marched back and forth, telling him everything that Martine had told her. It was ironic, he thought. The boss's daughter coming to him, the mechanic's son, for help. But what was even more ironic was the fact that it didn't really seem strange to him at all. It felt perfectly natural. The moon was in the sky. The river flowed to the sea. And Frances Kellerman turned to him when she had a problem – just as, he suddenly realized, he would want to turn to her if he had a problem.

'So, anyway,' Baby was saying, 'I thought, you know, that you might have a different perspective or something.' She threw her hands up in the air. 'I've gone over and over it, but I just don't know what to do.'

Johnny got to his feet, crossing the porch and standing in front of her. He put his hands on her shoulders and looked into her eyes. 'OK, Baby,' he said quietly, 'listen very carefully to what I'm gonna say, all right? 'Cause I'm only gonna say it once. Ready?'

She put on a look of great concentration. 'Ready.'

'OK. Do . . . not . . . do . . . anything.'

She was sure she must have misunderstood him. 'What?'

'You heard me.' He gave her a little shake. 'Nothing. As in not a thing.'

'But, Johnny. We've got to do *something*.'

'*We*?' He pointed to himself. 'Who's *we*, white woman? *We*, and especially *you*, don't have to do bubkes. You understand? The way I see it, this is nobody's business but Sweets' and Martine's.'

Baby grabbed hold of his hand. 'But that's just the point, Johnny. It is nobody else's business. But it's because of everybody else that they can't get together.'

'Baby—'

'Johnny, they're in love. They're really in love.'

She was squeezing his hand so tightly you'd think she was never going to let go. And it wasn't just her voice that was pleading, it was her eyes as well. He stared into them, feeling as though he were falling through space. Abruptly, he pulled away. 'Sometimes, y'know, Baby, love isn't enough.'

She grabbed hold again. 'Yes it is, Johnny.'

'No, Baby, it's not.'

'But it's got to be. Sweets and Martine have as much right to be together as me and – as anybody else does.'

'No, it doesn't gotta be enough, Baby. We're not livin' in some fairy tale. There are things in this world that are bigger than what two people feel for each other. You're not stupid, Baby. Get real. Martine's white and Sweets is a Negro. That's not some little thing you can just overlook, you know.'

She let go of him, turning her back. 'That's what Robin said.'

'Well, for once Robin's right.'

She kicked at the railing. 'But it's not fair. It's—'

'Fair? What are y'talkin' about, "fair"? Baby, there are places in this country where it would be illegal for Sweets and Martine to get married. Do you realize that? Do you realize that there are places in this country where colored people can't vote, or take a drink of water from a fountain, or go into a restaurant for something to eat? Places where they can't go to a decent school, where they have to sit at the back of the bus? Where they're being killed for standing up for their rights? Do you think that's "fair", Frances Kellerman? Huh? Do you think that's fair?'

'Of course I don't,' she said in a whisper, her voice shaking and close to tears. 'You know I don't. That's the sort of thing I want to see changed, that's what I want to fight against.' She snuffled back a tear as two warm, strong hands touched her shoulders.

'Aw, Baby,' said Johnny in the most tender voice she'd ever heard him use, 'don't cry. Get mad, but don't cry.' He brushed a strand of hair from her face. 'I know how you feel, I really do. But you've got to face the facts. There are some things that aren't gonna change overnight.'

She leaned against him, so close she could almost hear the beating of his heart. 'But if we . . . if ordinary people don't change things in their own lives then everything will always stay the same. It's only when people take risks that things change. If Sweets and Martine really want to be together then they'll tell everybody else to jump in the lake.'

His hands fell away and he moved beside her. For a few minutes he didn't say anything. A sadness she had never seen before came into his eyes as he stared up at the starry, starry night. 'Baby,' he said at last, his voice strangely quiet, 'this is real life. Not a story where everybody lives happily ever after.'

'But if they really love each other—'

'My old granny's got a saying,' said Johnny, pale in the moonlight. 'Love and a quarter will get you on the subway.'

Four

If you had asked Max Kellerman what the first thought was that came into Johnny Castle's mind each morning, Max would have said one of three things: food, cars, or girls. 'Boys like that,' Max would have said, 'what else do you think they think about all the time? It's either their stomachs, their Chevys, or their, you know, their hormones.'

But the truth was that, for the past few days at least, the first thought that had come into Johnny's mind when he woke up was the same as the last thing he thought about as he fell asleep: Jack Benny. Well, not Jack Benny exactly. What had been preoccupying Johnny was the new routine he was working on to perform the weekend Benny came up to Kellerman's. It had to be special, really special. He wanted to make Max notice just how good he and the other dancers were. How professional, how imaginative, how innovative. He wanted people to remember the night not just because Jack Benny had told a few jokes he or someone else had probably told a hundred times before, but because Johnny Castle had done the choreography.

This morning, however, Johnny opened his eyes just as dawn broke over the Catskills, dance steps and famous comedians far from his thoughts. He leaned over to check the time on the alarm clock, then fell back against the pillow with a sigh. Sweets. Sweets and Martine. He closed his eyes. He'd had this crazy dream. It had been straight out of *West Side Story*, and yet it had seemed so real. His heart was still pounding.

The dream had taken place in a school yard. In the center of the yard there was a house. It was an average, ordinary sort of house, with a front porch and a garage and a driveway. It had a television antenna on the roof and a bird feeder out front. It looked nice. Like a real family lived in it. He remembered thinking, that's a nice house, I wouldn't mind living there. There was an electric mower and a kid's bike on the lawn. And he could see into the house. It was that kind of dream. He could see the living room and the kitchen and the bedrooms. He could see the magazines on the coffee table and the jar of peanut butter and the used knife on the formica counter near the sink. The only unusual thing about the house was that it was sitting in the middle of a basketball court. And that on either side of the house, at different ends of the school yard, were two gangs. The Sharks and the Jets. The Sharks were surrounding Sweets. The Jets were surrounding Martine. Music was playing. Sweets and Martine were trying to get to the house. It was their house. And if they could get to the house they'd be safe. They'd be together. Everything would be all right. But the gangs wouldn't let them get to the house. Every time they took a step forward someone yanked them back. Or blocked their way. Or waved a knife in their faces.

'Why are you doing this to them?' Johnny wanted to yell. But it was a dream and no one could hear him. The music got louder and louder. Sweets was bleeding from the lip. Martine was struggling against these guys who were holding her. She was calling to Sweets. He was punching wildly, but he was more than outmatched. Martine broke free and started running towards the house. The door was open. She was screaming his name. He was fighting his way nearer and nearer to the house. The music changed. It was Ben E. King singing 'Stand By Me'. And suddenly, instead of Martine running towards the house, it was Baby. 'Johnny!' she was shouting. 'Johnny! Johnny! You've got to try! You can't give up!' And she was right, it wasn't Sweets at all getting the crap kicked out of him by the Sharks. It was him. 'Johnny!' Baby screamed as she jumped on to the porch. 'Johnny! Run! Run!'

Safe in his bed, with the alarm clock ticking and the early light slipping in under the blinds, Johnny opened his eyes again. And wondered what Sweets and Martine were going to do.

Sweets glanced up as the kitchen door opened and Johnny walked in. He reached for another cup. 'You're up early, man,' he said over his shoulder.

'Me?' Johnny watched Sweets' hand shake as he poured out two cups of fresh coffee. He looked about ten times worse than Johnny felt. 'I thought it was against your religion to get up before lunch time.'

Sweets smiled. It was a smile as false as Johnny's grandmother's teeth. 'Yeah, well . . .' he mumbled, 'I couldn't sleep. You know, too hot.'

Johnny nodded. 'Yeah, I know. I couldn't sleep either.'

Sweets picked up his cup. 'What say we take these out on the verandah? Catch the last of the sunrise.'

'So,' said Johnny, once they were both leaning against the rail, looking out towards the mountains where the sky was still tinged with gold.

'So,' said Sweets.

'Looks like we're in for another scorcher,' said Johnny.

Sweets nodded. 'Yeah, it sure does.'

'It must be murder in the city,' said Johnny.

'Yeah,' agreed Sweets, 'it must be murder.'

Johnny tapped his foot. The birds chirped and chattered. Sweets kept his eyes fixed on the distance.

'So you couldn't sleep either, huh?' said Johnny.

'No,' said Sweets.

Johnny looked over at him. He had seen Sweets after an all-night jam. And he'd seen him after a night of celebrating a Yankees' victory. But he hadn't ever seen him look this rough. Where Johnny came from, you didn't talk much about personal problems. Women did. Women were always getting involved in everybody else's lives, but not men. Men kept to themselves. If a buddy of yours had a bad time – if he'd just gotten drafted or his girlfriend had left him or something like that – you might take him out for a couple of beers, but you wouldn't expect him to say a lot. You wouldn't expect him to tell you how he really really felt. Johnny turned back to the mountains, looking brand-new in the morning sunshine. Where he came from was what he was trying to escape, wasn't it? He took a deep breath. 'You wanna talk about it?' he asked in a rush.

Sweets didn't blink. 'Talk about what?'

Johnny shrugged. 'You know . . .'

Sweets leaned forward. 'Yeah, I know. What I don't know is how you know.'

'Well, we were all there last night . . . I mean, it doesn't take much to put one and one together and—'

'You've been talkin' to Baby, right?' He didn't wait for Johnny to reply but went on. 'The trouble with Baby is she thinks everything's possible in this world. But you and me,' said Sweets, glancing over at the young man staring into his empty coffee cup, 'you and me, we know that's not true.'

'Yeah,' agreed Johnny, 'we know that . . . but—'

'There ain't no buts,' said Sweets quickly. 'Let me tell you a little story, okay? It's about this young colored guy, right? Now this guy is an ace musician. He can play the guitar. He can play the piano. He plays, he writes, he arranges. He's not the best, maybe, but he's real real good. Only thing he needs is a chance, right? Just one chance. And this audition comes up for this very famous band. They're goin' on a nationwide tour and they're lookin' for a new piano player. Our colored kid, he's been playing clubs and bars since he was old enough to get in the door, and he knows he's hot.' He paused for a second, watching the sky. 'You know what I mean, Johnno? Really hot.'

Johnny nodded, not looking around.

'So he goes to this audition. He pushes his way in and he gets a hearing and he's terrific. But he doesn't get the job. He doesn't get the job because this band is not about to go on a nationwide tour with a colored piano player. What happens when they get to Atlanta? Or even Minneapolis? What happens when they want to go in for a meal or get a hotel for the night?'

'Yeah, but Sweets, that was a while ago. Things are changin'—'

'They're not changin' that much. I had the talent for that job, Johnny, but I couldn't have it because I wasn't the right color. I would've caused too much trouble. And as far as I can see, Martine's just like that job.'

'Yeah, but Sweets, maybe if—'

'And y'know what else? I wonder a lot what would've happened if they'd offered me that job. If I'd really thought about everything that was involved, would I've taken it? And if I had, then what? How long before it got too much for me? Or too much for the rest of the band? How long before they started hatin' me and I started hatin' them?'

'But if they'd really wanted you . . . if they'd been willin' to take the risks . . .'

Sweets stood up straight. 'I don't wanna talk about it any more.'

Johnny was looking at the beautiful Kellerman's view, the view families came back for year after year, but what he was seeing was that stupid dream. Martine running for the house. Baby shouting to him.

'Look, Sweets,' he said, groping for the right words, 'I know this is none of my business—'

'You said it,' said Sweets. 'It's none of your business.'

Johnny tried again. 'Yeah, well, it's not like I'm trying to interfere or anything.'

Sweets was starting to walk away. 'Then don't.'

Johnny swung around in exasperation. 'Will you at least give me a chance to say what I wanna say? I mean, you've talked me through one or two things, and I've appreciated that.'

Sweets stopped in the doorway. 'And I appreciate what you're tryin' to do, really, but, believe me, Johnny, this is different.'

Johnny, the morning behind him, watched Sweets walk into the darkness of the hotel. One of the voices in his head was saying, 'Sweets is right. It is different.' But another voice, one that sounded suspiciously like Frances Kellerman, was saying, 'What are you talking about, "different"? It's all part of the same life, isn't it?'

'Robin,' Baby was saying as they walked past the shady grove where Penny was teaching an eager group of middle-aged couples how to do the hokey-pokey and towards the pool, 'I thought you promised you wouldn't tell anybody about Sweets and Martine.'

'I didn't,' said Robin, looking shocked. 'Who would I tell?'

'Well, I don't know,' said Baby, 'but it's not even time for lunch and half the staff seems to know.'

Robin came to a sudden stop and put her hands on her hips. 'Who, Baby? You have to substantiate your allegations. Who knows?'

Baby held up one hand and started ticking names off on her fingers. 'Norman.'

'Oh, Norman,' Robin waved the name away. 'I just happened to run into him on my way to calisthenics. He brought it up first, Baby. Really. I told him my lips were sealed, but he forced it out of me.'

Baby seemed unconvinced. 'Oh, sure, Norman Bryant, the Russians' secret weapon. The KGB uses him when they have spies they can't make talk.'

'Really, Baby. You know how persistent Norman can be.'

'Sherry.'

Robin looked over towards the hokey-pokeyers. They were shaking it to the left, and shaking it to the right, seeming to be having the time of their lives. She wished, all of a sudden, that she was lined up with them, and not standing here being grilled by Baby. 'Sherry? Well, Sherry brought me my breakfast, and you know how it is. One minute you're talking about the eggs and the next minute—'

'Penny.'

'Penny?'

'Yeah, Penny. You remember Penny. Did she bring you your breakfast, too?'

'Nooo. She came over to me while I was doing my deep knee-bends. You know what a bully she is, Baby. It's because she grew up on the streets. I wouldn't be surprised if she owns a knife. And anyway, she wouldn't leave me alone until I'd told her everything I knew.'

'Andy.'

Robin held up her hands. 'Oh, no, Frances Kellerman, you can't get me for Andy. He must've overheard me talking to Arlene—'

'Arlene? You even told the chambermaid?'

'Well, I—'

'Oh, Robin, what am I going to do with you?' Baby wondered why she even bothered getting upset. She'd known this was going to happen. She should probably be grateful that she hadn't woken up to Robin telling the story of Sweets and Martine over the PA system.

'I don't know what you're getting so upset about,' said Robin, in the same tone she'd used when she had the little accident last spring with her father's car. 'Everybody's very sympathetic.' This news seemed to make Baby feel as good as the information that the other car looked worse than theirs had made her father feel.

'Oh, great!' Baby threw her hands in the air. 'Well, everything's all right then. Maybe you could arrange to have everybody sing "Somewhere" after supper. That should cheer Sweets up.'

'I don't know what you're getting so sarcastic about, Baby,' said Robin. 'You're the one who wanted to help Martine. Surely getting everybody on her side is one way of doing that. If Sweets sees that they've got support—'

Baby held up her hand. 'Wait a minute, Robin. I thought you were the one who said I shouldn't interfere. I thought you were the one who said Sweets being colored and Martine being white wasn't a little difference you could overlook.'

'What can I say?' asked Robin with a shrug. 'I dreamed about *West Side Story* all night long. And anyway,' she grinned, 'you know I've always been a hopeless romantic.'

Martine Jellico was sitting in a chair by the edge of the pool, not far from where she and Sweets had been sitting the night before. But instead of the moonlight and the stars and the unhappy-looking couple staring back at her from the water, there was now only sunshine and blue skies and dozens of people splashing in the pool. And beside her, instead of Sweets, being distant and moody, was Max Kellerman, chatting happily away to her about his wife.

'You'll like Elizabeth,' Max was saying, 'and she'll like you. Plus,' he winked, 'she could turn out to be a good customer. She's going to need a lot of books for this college course she's taking.'

Martine touched his hand. 'You must really be proud of her, Max.'

Max flushed. 'Well, I wasn't too proud at first, if you want to know the truth. I reacted like part of the reactionary male establishment when she first told me.' He gave her a smile that on a man with more hair and less tummy would have been boyish. 'But I'm pretty proud of her now. She sort of convinced me that you have to move with the times.'

Martine's own smile evaporated like a drop of water in the sun. 'I wish you'd tell that to Sweets,' she said quietly.

Max watched a small boy run up to the edge of the diving board, stretch out his arms, close his eyes, leap – and belly-whop into the pool. 'So that is why you're here.'

Martine nodded. 'I know you've got the best corned beef this side of Second Avenue, Max, but, yes, I came because of Sweets.'

Max brushed a fly away. 'I was actually hoping it was the fresh air and the chance to brush up on your basket weaving.'

Martine caught the seriousness in his voice. 'Hoping?'

Max turned his eyes to her. 'Yes, hoping. I'd sort of had the impression that everything was settled between you two—'

The warm, friendly atmosphere that had been between them went the way of her smile. All at once they might have been sitting on an ice floe in Alaska, watching the penguins diving for fish. 'You mean you think I've made a mistake coming after him? What happened to moving with the times?'

Max sighed. Why was it, he wondered, that all women jumped to conclusions? And why was it that when they jumped to these conclusions, they all got exactly the same incredulous tone in their voices? Every woman he knew – from his mother to his wife to his daughter to Martine Jellico – had the ability to make him feel like either an idiot or some sort of tyrant. 'It's not a question of what I think, Martine,' he said, as patient and reasonable as ever. 'It's just that Sweets . . . that the two of you went through a lot before and I'm not sure that the situation's changed any—'

Martine was feeling underneath her chair for her sandals. 'I can see you and Sweets have already been through all this.'

'Whoa, Martine, whoa.' Max laid a hand on her arm. 'The only thing Sweets has said to me since he walked off with you last night is "Sorry". We haven't talked about it at all.'

She snapped on her shoes. 'But you've still made your mind up.'

Helpless, that's how women made him feel. Completely helpless. Helpless and wrong. No matter what he said. No matter what he did. No matter how good his intentions. He was about to defend himself when, just beyond her, he saw two more women heading towards them. From the bright, eager smiles on their faces he could tell they weren't going to make him feel any better.

He could tell from the way their eyes went straight to Martine that they were already on a crusade. Batman and Robin. 'Oh, boy,' said Max with a shake of his head. He looked up at the sky, a feeling of premonition grabbing his heart. 'What have I done to deserve this?' he asked out loud. Martine turned around quickly. She thought he was talking to her. But he wasn't. He was talking to God.

Five

Max, Baby and Robin stood by the side of the pool, watching Martine Jellico as she marched purposefully past the sunbathers and the pleasant grove where Penny's hokey-pokey class was just breaking up. A photograph taken of the three of them right then would have caught what looked like a moment of perfect family bliss. Baby on one side, smiling. Robin on the other side, smiling. And Max in the middle, his arms stretched proudly around their shoulders, grinning away like a man who wanted no more from life than to have his favorite daughter and his favorite niece by his side. But photographs, of course, do lie.

No sooner was Martine out of sight and hearing than Max rounded on his favorite daughter and his favorite niece, fighting hard to keep his smile up and his voice down in front of his guests. 'You two,' he hissed, 'I want you to swear to me that you won't interfere anymore, or I'm sending both of you home on the first bus.'

'Now, Dad,' said Baby, 'I really think you're over-reacting.'

'Anymore?' asked Robin.

'No talk,' said Max. 'Just promise.'

The first thing Martine had done when Baby and Robin joined them was turn to Baby and say,

'Your father's trying to convince me to give up.' Both Baby and Robin had immediately turned on him, looking as though they'd just found out that he went around kicking dogs and stealing candy from young children. 'How could you!' their young, trusting eyes seemed to shout at him. Baby had called Martine 'Marty'. 'Oh, Marty,' she'd said. 'I don't believe this!'

The conversation that followed was all about fighting for true love, standing up for your beliefs, and striking a blow for personal freedom. Max wasn't asked to join in this conversation. In fact, it was quite clear from the sharp little glances all three of them gave him every now and then that they considered him to be the enemy of true love, liberty, and the rights of the individual. Him! Max Kellerman! The man who still remembered what his wife was wearing the first time he met her. The man who brought moonlight dancing to the Catskills. The man whose favorite song was 'My Way'. They were probably already calling him Stalin behind his back.

'But, Dad,' said Baby. 'Be reasonable. We haven't done anything.'

'Yet, you mean,' snarled Max. 'And you're not going to, if I have anything to say about it.'

'But I never even met Martine before,' protested Robin.

Max glared at her. 'Well, you seem to know an awful lot about her life for someone who never met her before.'

Robin looked guilty. And then she looked at Baby.

Max looked at Baby.

Baby looked at Amy Wallenstein. Amy Wallenstein was floating in the shallow end of the pool on a pink and purple sea horse. 'Well,' she said carefully, 'we – me and Martine – we did have a little talk last night. You know, when I was helping her get settled . . .'

'Oh, really, Uncle Max,' Robin butted in, 'you can't be mad at us for being on her side, can you? I mean, if this isn't the most romantic thing you've ever heard . . .'

'It's not a question of romance,' said Max. 'And it's certainly not a question of sides—'

'But you do think she should go back to the city, don't you?' cut in Baby. 'You think she should just turn her back on the man she loves and live a lie for the rest of her life.'

He was a practical, down-to-earth businessman, a man with a strong sense of reality. She must get this tendency toward melodrama from her mother's side of the family. 'What I think,' said Max, 'is that you two should mind your own business for once in your lives.'

'I agree with you, Mr Kellerman,' said Neil, suddenly materializing beside them. He leaned over and whispered loudly into Baby's ear, 'And I think at least some of your business should be me.'

Robin groaned.

Baby kicked him.

Normally, this was just the sort of thing Max wanted to hear, but today even the prospect of Baby dating a pre-med student couldn't cheer him up. 'For God's sake, Neil,' he said shortly. 'Why aren't you at your station?'

Neil grinned. 'I'm patrolin'.'

'Neil, this is an average-size pool area, not the South Vietnam jungle. You don't have to patrol it. You just have to sit in your chair and watch out that no-one drowns.'

Neil pointed to himself with not a hint of modesty. 'Hey, Mr K,' he said, showing every tooth in his head, 'I'm a professional. I don't believe in shortcuts.'

Max could see this developing into one of Neil's forty-minute oral autobiographies. How I Made My Parents The Happiest Parents In The World. How I Was The Youngest Eagle Scout In History. How I Saved The Track Team From Ignominy. Neil was a nice boy, especially compared to some Jersey gigolos Max could think of, but once you'd heard how the high school football coach cried when Neil went off to college you really didn't have to hear it again. 'That's very nice Neil. Now if you'll excuse us—'

But Neil was already launched. Much to everyone's surprise, however, he wasn't talking about himself. 'I saw you talkin' to Sweets' lady,' he was saying.

Three heads turned towards him. 'How the heck . . .' spluttered Max.

Neil put a hand on Max's shoulder. 'You know, I like Sweets a lot, Mr K, he's a great guy and all, but, man to man . . .' He looked over at Baby. 'Man to man, I sort of think people should stick to their own kind, don't you?'

Baby clenched her hands into fists. 'You would say that!' she raged.

'Hey, Baby, it's only sensible.' He patted Max's shoulder. 'I'm sure your father agrees with me. He wouldn't want you runnin' off with some Russian or something, would you, Mr K? He'd want you to find someone who was, you know, just like you.'

'Well, in that case,' said Robin pleasantly, 'you'd better start looking for the slug of your dreams.'

* * *

The last of the hokey-pokeyers, flushed and exhausted but filled with a deep sense of accomplishment, were just limping away as Johnny came loping across the grass to where Penny was closing up the record player. 'Rid your mind of all thoughts of the hokey-pokey and the bunny hop,' he laughed. He gave her a playful hug. 'I want you to come with me and practise some new steps I've worked out for next weekend's routine.'

Penny threw her towel at him. 'Can't you give me a five-minute break? I've been doing this for hours. Kellerman should gave me combat pay. My feet are black and blue and my back's killin' me. When I close my eyes I see nothing in front of me but Mrs Schwartz in her purple mumu, doin' the hokey-pokey with all her might.' She collapsed on the lawn with a groan. 'I'm just about all hoked out.'

He sat down next to her. 'OK, Pen, OK. I'm no slave driver, you know that.' He looked at his watch. 'You've got exactly five minutes. Starting now.'

'Very fun— Hey,' she said, her attention distracted by something behind him, 'isn't that Sweets' lady? She looks pretty determined.'

Johnny didn't turn around. 'What are you talkin' about, "Sweets' lady"?' he asked offhandedly.

Penny gave him a look. 'Whatta y'think I am, stupid?' She punched his arm. 'I saw her when she suddenly turned up last night and he forgot he was playin' the piano. Come on,' she coaxed. 'I know you know somethin' . . .'

He examined the toe of his sneaker as though it was the most interesting thing in the world.

'Penny, I don't know what you're talkin' about. Honest. As far as I know, she's just an old friend.' He gave her his most charming how-can-you-doubt-what-I'm-saying grin. 'Sweets does have a lot of friends, you know.'

What was it with guys? You knew them for years. You worked with them. You listened to their complaints and their plans. You comforted them when they had a fight with their old man or some old windbag made them feel about two inches tall. You nursed them when they had flu or they sprained a tendon. And then what? And then they acted like you didn't know them at all. That they could fool you with just a smile. 'And I saw them go off together.' She snapped her fingers. '*And* I saw how he looked when he came back.'

Johnny lay back on the grass. 'Pen, please, we're talkin' a hundred per cent circumstantial evidence here. You don't know anything. You don't know who she is. You don't know why she came up here. You sure don't know how Sweets felt when he got back to the band last night.'

'But you do,' she persisted.

'No, I don't. All I know is that he was probably bored out of his gourd at the thought of having to play "Chicago" for that awful guy again.'

Penny leaned over him, smiling like a prom queen. '*And* I talked to Robin this morning,' she said sweetly.

Johnny closed his eyes. 'I should of known.'

'That's what the princess wanted to talk to you about last night, isn't it.'

'Penny—'

'Is that why you never came back in to dance? 'Cause you went to talk to Sweets?'

'No, Penny, that's not why I—'

'But you have talked t'him, haven't you? I just know you have.' She shook his arm. 'Come on, Johnny, you can tell me. What's gonna happen? Is Sweets gonna marry her, you think?'

Johnny and Max thought of themselves as being as alike as tutti-frutti ice cream and the duck billed platypus. But in reality they had quite a bit in common. For Johnny, like Max, was often perplexed by female behavior. What was it with women anyway, he wondered? A man could work with another man for half a dozen years and never know whether the other guy was married or divorced or if he had his own teeth. But put two women together for five minutes and they knew everything about each other from their bra sizes to the names of their unborn children. 'Penny, this really isn't anybody's business but Sweets',' he said.

Penny looked at him with a mixture of shrewdness and jealousy. 'Oh, yeah? And is that what you told Little Miss Peace Corps? That it wasn't any of her business? You were out on the porch with her an awful long time for such a short message.'

Johnny propped himself up on his elbows. 'Yes, as a matter of fact, that was what I told her. But obviously she didn't listen to me either.'

Penny stared down at the healthy, well-tended and regularly weeded Kellerman lawn. 'Not even when you put your arms around her?'

No wonder guys went into the army. All you had to deal with in the army was people trying to shoot you or blow you up. It must be so uncomplicated. 'Penny, I didn't—look, could we have one argument at a time here?'

For several seconds Penny concentrated on pulling up innocent clumps of grass. Ever since she'd talked to Robin this morning something had been bothering her. It wasn't exactly the fact that Sweets was colored and Martine was white. It was more the idea that that fact shouldn't separate them. That with so much keeping them apart they might still be able to get together. Because if two people could cross those tracks, what was there to stop two other people from crossing another set of tracks? 'Yeah, but Johnny,' she ventured at last. 'Whatta y'really think? Do you think they should get together?'

'Oh, I think they should get together, definitely,' came the enthusiastic reply.

Johnny, certain that he hadn't opened his mouth yet, looked up in surprise. And sure enough, there was Norm, Pollyanna in a Kellerman's uniform, bobbing his head up and down and grinning madly.

'I'm always on the side of true love,' said Norman.

'Geez,' sighed Johnny, 'I should of known.'

An even more wistful expression than usual came over Norman's face. 'Don't you guys agree?' He spread his arms open wide. 'Love makes the world go round.'

'Centripetal force makes the world go round,' said Johnny.

'I don't know,' said Penny. 'I mean, I'm all in favor of true love an' everything . . .' She glanced over at Johnny. He was lying back on the grass, pretending to ignore them. 'But you know what they say, love is blind. And maybe when people are too different . . . you know . . . well, maybe people should just stick t'their own kind.'

Johnny shut his eyes tight, slipping on his sunglasses at the same time.

'Well, I'm not so sure about that,' said Norman. 'I know I've only been out on three dates in my life. And two of them were with my cousin Flo. And I guess you'd have to say that she is my own kind. I mean, she's got the Bryant ears, and we go to the same dentist, and she's allergic to clams just like me . . .' He appealed to Penny, the only other person who seemed to be awake. 'But doesn't being in love with someone sort of make them your own kind?'

Penny gave him one of the dirtiest looks he'd ever seen. Max Kellerman should have been taking lessons from her. 'What sorta stupid thing is that to say?' she snapped at him. 'Of course it doesn't. You think if somebody who's rich loves somebody who's poor, it makes them equal? You think Martine loving Sweets makes him white?'

'Well, no, that's not what I meant,' muttered Norman. 'I just meant that, you know . . .' he floundered to a halt. 'Don't you know what I mean?'

'No,' said Penny, getting to her feet, 'I don't know what you mean.'

'Johnny?' pleaded Norman. 'Don't you know what I mean?'

The sun was reflecting off Johnny's glasses like stars. 'Maybe,' he said, his voice almost drowned by the sound of delighted squeals coming from the pool area. 'Maybe. I'm not sure.'

It was high noon. High noon and a sudden quiet had fallen over Kellerman's resort. The croquet field was empty. The hula-hoop competition had been abandoned, one yellow hoop left on its own in the grass. Even the shuffle-board court lay silent in the blistering sun. One lone figure walked along the path to the staff quarters. Slowly. Haltingly. Counting every step of this, the longest walk of her life. The walk that was taking her to the big showdown. She might not come back alive.

But though the figure was all alone, she was being watched by half a dozen pairs of eyes. By Max at his office window; by Penny and Norman from the doorway of her cabin; by Johnny from a nearby hill; by Baby and Robin from the parking lot that bordered on the staff area. Each of them thinking their own thoughts. Each of them holding their breath.

OK, Martine, Martine was telling herself as she got nearer and nearer to Sweets' cabin, you came all the way up here to talk to this man and you can't back down now. The tray she was carrying shook in her hands. Her heart was pounding away like the hooves of stampeding cattle. Why had she thought this was all going to be so easy? Why had she thought that all she needed to do was tell Sweets that she'd changed her mind and all would be forgiven, bells would ring, fireworks would go off in the sky, and everything would be just the way it should be? Why hadn't it occurred to her that he might not want to know about it? That he would go into hiding and refuse to confront her?

She checked the cabin number Baby had written down for her and then stared warily at the door in front of her. It was definitely the same number. She looked at it again. Yes, it was hard to confuse the number five. She took a deep breath. Your mother didn't raise any cowardly children, she reminded herself. She knocked. Then she knocked again – this time loudly enough so that anyone inside would be able to hear it. Then, encouraged by the sound, she knocked even harder.

'Who is it?' called that old familiar voice.

Martine's heart did a somersault. 'Room service!' she called brightly.

The sudden knocking on the door startled Sweets out of the reverie he'd been for the past few hours. Every once and a while he'd look at the clock and tell himself that he couldn't stay in here forever, he'd have to go out and find Martine. But then the fight he'd been having with himself since the night before would begin again. The two sides of him seemed to be equally matched. One minute he was sure that the thing to do was to marry Martine; the next he was sure that it wasn't. Go to her. Stay here. Give it a chance. You'll only get hurt again. You love each other, you can make it. You love each other, but you can't make it. We already tried. You didn't try enough. If I don't marry her now I'll always regret it. If I do marry her now we'll both regret it. And then someone started pounding on the door like the place was on fire.

'Who is it?' he shouted. He jumped off the bed. Room service? He hadn't ordered any room service. The only time he'd ever had room service at Kellerman's was the time he had the Asian flu. He jerked the door open. 'Martine.'

'Who were you expecting, the Marx Brothers?'

'Martine, I—'

She held up the tray. 'You going to ask me in, or would you rather have a picnic out on the lawn?'

Instinctively, he looked behind her to see if she was being watched. But there was nothing behind her but trees. Trees and sunshine. 'Come in. Come in.' He stood back to let her enter, taking one last look towards the main building before he slammed the door shut. 'Look, Martine, I'm sorry I—'

She walked into the room as though she belonged there. She put the tray down on his desk. 'It's OK, Sweets. I know I sort of took you by surprise.' She looked around, taking everything in – the empty glass on the night table, the rumpled bed, the photograph of the two of them in the snow in Washington Square Park, laughing like maniacs. 'Is it OK if I sit?'

'Yeah, sure.' He gestured to the only chair.

She sat on the bed.

He stayed on his feet. The fifteen hours or so that he'd had to get used to the idea of her again hadn't been enough. If he'd thought that staying away from her would make him stronger when he did face her, he'd been wrong. His heart was racing and his knees felt weak. It was impossible for him to take his eyes off her.

'Well,' she said, with false brightness. She was surprised to find that she was holding on to the spread as though she were afraid of falling off. 'Here we are!'

He didn't smile back. 'You know, Martine, you could cause some grief, coming here like this.'

She made a little face. 'So what? It's caused *me* a lot more grief not coming here.'

He tried to laugh, but it sounded more like he was choking. '*So what*? That's a change of tune, isn't it?'

She was kneading the regulation blue-and-green plaid cover between her thin, long fingers, and refusing to meet his eyes. 'Yeah. Yeah, it's a change of tune. But I've done a lot of thinking lately. And maybe you were right before when you said that if other people had trouble with us that was their problem.'

He sat down on the chair. 'But I've done a lot of thinking, too Martine. And maybe you were right when you said they would only destroy us in the end . . . that there wouldn't be anything left.'

She looked at him then, her large, dark eyes holding him in place. But there is something left, Sweets. Don't tell me there isn't. The minute I saw you last night I knew I hadn't been wrong. You still love me. I know you do.'

It was like being shot at close range. He could hardly speak. 'I never said I'd stop loving you, babe, I—'

She was standing in front of him so quickly that he didn't even see her move. She knelt down so they were level. 'Then let's go back to the way it was. You and me. Only this time let's do it for keeps.'

'Martine, we can't pretend that what happened to us didn't happen. We had a rough time. You couldn't've forgotten it, Martine. It was making a wreck out of you and a very unnice person out of me. And that was in New York City.' He cleared his throat. 'You were the one who wanted to end it, Martine. You were . . .' His voice trailed off as he remembered the scenes they'd had. The nights he'd stay out jamming all night rather than have to face her tears. 'If you couldn't handle it—'

She took hold of his hands. 'But that was two years ago, honey. I'm older now.' She smiled. 'And tougher.'

'You don't look tough, babe,' he breathed. 'You look like an angel.'

'My skin's a lot thicker than it used to be.'

He looked down at the hands holding his. 'But just as white.'

'And just as soft.'

'Martine—'

'Just give me another chance, that's all I'm asking. One more shot. Right here and now. If I can handle it at Kellerman's, then I can handle it anywhere . . . and any time.'

How many nights had he lain awake, dreaming of this moment . . . torturing himself with maybes and might-have-beens? How many times had he rung her number, wanting to beg her to come back to him – and then hung up before she could answer the phone?

'And what about Mark?' he asked at last.

She was moving towards him, closer and closer. 'We both know what I really want,' she whispered. 'The question is, what about you?'

All those words, Sweets thought to himself as his lips found hers. All those words, years and years and years of words, and in the end this kiss was all either of them had ever needed.

Six

In more philosophical moments, Max sometimes likened Kellerman's to a small town. It was pleasant and peaceful. It had a lot of greenery. The crime rate was low. It provided everything any reasonable person could want, from golf shoes and the latest magazines to gefilte fish and butterscotch sundaes.

And it was friendly. Everyone knew everyone else, at least by sight. They greeted you as you went in for breakfast. They waved at you across the volleyball net. They asked after your sunburn as they pedaled by on one of the paddle boats. In New York City you could go for days, even weeks, without ever meeting someone you knew. But not in Small Town America. And not at Kellerman's. 'It's like living in *The Music Man,*' Max had been heard to comment on more than one occasion, usually after a strong martini. 'Half the time I expect to step out of my office and find everyone standing in the forecourt, singing.'

But what Max always failed to mention in these philosophical moments was that if Kellerman's had all the virtues of a small town, it also had the vices. You couldn't find a deli open at twelve in the morning. You didn't have a choice of movies. There was no good Chinese restaurant within forty miles. The local radio stations didn't play Little Richard or Chuck Berry. You wouldn't find *The Catcher in the Rye* in the book rack of the newspaper concession. There was no such thing as privacy. Even with so much going on – hat-making contests and tennis lessons, golf games and special coaching sessions, swimming and dancing and bird-watching walks – people always found the time to keep an eye on one another. When Mr and Mrs Bower had the fight about which one of them had lost the bridge tournament, the rest of the guests had already picked sides before Mr Bower had had time to put the Band Aid on his forehead. Half of Kellerman's knew Laverne Waterman was going to frost her hair before she did, and the other half had an opinion on it before they saw the results. Poolside conversation consisted of comments on the day's menu, advice on tanning or dieting, the solution to finding world peace and how to get ahead in business, and updates of the private lives of staff and guests alike. 'Did you know his father's buying him a Corvette when he graduates college?' 'Did you know she wears a girdle?' 'Did you hear she had her nose fixed?' 'I have it on good authority that he's been investigated by the IRS.' 'I wouldn't buy a used car from him, either.' 'You think those aren't implants?' 'Mafia? Of course he's got Mafia connections. You think he's so fond of spaghetti by accident?' 'Well, I don't care what she told you. The maid said she came up with thirty-six pairs of shoes!'

It was unlikely, then, that anything as newsworthy and controversial as Sweets and Martine should have gone unnoticed for much more than a nanosecond. As soon as they stepped into the bright Catskill sunshine the heads began turning.

Martine squeezed Sweets' hand as they walked towards the main building. 'Everybody's looking at us,' she said. As though he hadn't noticed.

'Then we oughta give them something to look at,' winked Sweets. He slipped his arm around her waist.

Mrs Schwartz, playing Scrabble with Mr Schwartz in the shade of their bungalow's porch, looked up just as Sweets and Martine passed by. 'Oh my God,' Mrs Schwartz gasped, clutching her ample bosom, 'I can't believe my eyes.'

Mr Schwartz, intent on getting rid of his 'z', didn't bother looking up. After all, he and Mrs Schwartz had been married for over thirty-five years. Her clutching her bosom could signify anything from an invasion of Cuba by the CIA to a glass ring on the dining table. 'What is it, dear?' he asked, with what might be mistaken as patience.

Mrs Schwartz opened and closed her mouth a few times. She blinked. Maybe Mr Schwartz was right, and she'd been taking too many of those sleeping pills the doctor'd prescribed. 'It's a mixed couple!' she finally managed to gasp. 'A mixed couple! Here at Kellerman's!'

He could make the word 'zoo', but it wouldn't get him even a double-letter score. On the other hand, if he made 'freezer' he'd get a triple-word score. All he needed was an 'e' and an 'r'. 'Bea,' he said, wondering if he should risk waiting for the 'e' and the 'r', 'all couples are mixed. That's the whole point. One's a man and the other's a woman.' He decided to settle for 'zoo'. 'Except in New York City, maybe.'

'Not that kind of mixed,' said Mrs Schwartz. She gestured across the lawn. '*That* kind of mixed.'

Mr Schwartz carefully laid down his letters. 'Seventeen points,' he sighed. Then he looked in the direction his wife was pointing. 'Isn't that the piano player?' he asked.

'Yes, that's the piano player,' hissed Mrs Schwartz, 'but look who he's with.'

Mr Schwartz looked. 'Oh,' nodded Mr Schwartz, '*that* kind of mixed.' He sipped his iced tea. 'Well, that should stir things up.'

'Stir things up?' repeated Mrs Schwartz. 'Is that all you can say? "Stir things up"? This is Kellerman's, Josh, not some club in the Village. This isn't a hangout for beatniks. Families come here.'

Mr Schwartz moved the sprig of mint that decorated his drink out of his left nostril. 'Well, that's pretty lucky then,' he said. 'Seeing as those two look like a family is exactly what they want to start.'

Mrs Schwartz wrote his score on the pad and threw the pencil down on the table. 'Seventeen points,' she snapped. 'What a waste of a "z".' She pointed to the side of the board. 'You should've waited for an "e" and an "r",' she said crisply. 'Then you could've made "freezer".'

Baby, on her way to work, was walking beside Max, who was on his way to a nervous breakdown.

'Oh, for Pete's sake, Dad,' Baby was saying, having to run a little just to keep up with him, 'it's not that bad. Nobody's started burning crosses on the lawn yet or anything.'

Max smirked. 'Thank you, honey, that's very comforting. It gives me something to look forward to. After all, it's only been a day. They haven't had a chance to turn violent.'

'So a couple of people have gone home early, so what? It's not the end of the world.'

'Frances,' said Max. Sometimes when he called her Frances it was a sign that he wanted her to know he considered her an adult. Other times it meant that if she weren't his daughter, whom he loved very much, he would have an overwhelming urge to strangle her. This was clearly one of the other times. 'Frances, I have Jack Benny coming up here next week. It's costing me a lot of money to have Benny. It'd be nice if he had someone to play to.'

'Oh, come on, Dad. The whole place isn't going to empty out just because Sweets and Martine hold hands in public. This *is* 1963, you know.'

'Frances,' said Max, 'Frances, I am running a hotel here, not a freedom march. This is all getting to be just a little too much for me.'

'But what about everything you always told me about prejudice and bigotry? What about America being the one country that was created so everybody could be equal and free? So that everybody could have a chance? Was that just talk? Didn't that mean anything?'

Max came to a sudden stop. He stood for a few minutes just looking into his daughter's eyes. This was the child they had named Frances, after the first woman in the cabinet. This was the child who was going to make the world a better place for everyone. This was the child he had always been so proud of – the one with the same principles and ideals he'd had when he was young. He looked into her eyes and it occurred to him that he still had those same principles and ideals, he'd just shoved them to one side, the way you sometimes did as you got older. 'Of course it meant something,' he said at last. 'I didn't mean to suggest that . . . I'm just worried, that's all.'

'You don't have to worry, Dad,' she said, giving him a hug. 'This is the Catskills, not Little Rock. Everything's under control.'

Johnny, sitting at the patio bar with two of his best mambo students, gave Baby a wink as she hurried by with a full tray. Baby didn't wink back. She had been sort of not speaking to Johnny since their talk about Sweets and Martine. She wasn't sure why, but every time she thought about that conversation it got her down. She'd just been so sure that he'd agree with her that love could conquer all. It had never occurred to her that he might have a different opinion. He was the guy who was always talking about fighting for what you wanted and standing up for yourself. He was supposed to believe in love. But instead of saying that of course Sweets and Martine had a right to be together he'd started going on about all the things standing in their way. That wasn't what she'd wanted to hear. Not from Johnny it wasn't. She could take it from Max. She could take it from Neil. She could take it from her Aunt Jackie, who once had a four-week migraine when her eldest daughter came home with a boy who wasn't Jewish. But not from Johnny.

'Working hard?' he called after her.

But she didn't deign to answer. She wanted him to know she was disappointed in him.

'It's too bad they can't air-condition the outdoors,' said Robin as Baby came over to her table. She fanned herself with her place mat. 'Then this place would be perfect. If they could also get rid of the flies.'

Baby laughed. 'I'll have a word with the management. See what they can do.' She started unloading her tray. 'Hey, Robin,' she said as she put the tunafish club sandwich, the order of fries, the bowl of coleslaw and the large cola on the table in front of her cousin. 'What ever happened to your diet?'

'My diet?' Robin lifted the top slice of bread. 'You think there's too much mayo in the tuna?' She looked at it critically. 'Maybe you should take it back and wash it.'

Baby shook her head in wonderment. 'You're too much, you know that? You've got a double portion of fries and a giant soda and you want me to wash the mayo out of the tuna salad? Are you nuts?'

Robin looked indignant. 'That just shows how much you know, Frances Kellerman,' said Robin. 'It just so happens that that's a diet soda, and if you use your eyes you'll see that I didn't order any ketchup with the fries, and anyway . . .' Robin's voice trailed off as she caught sight of something or someone behind Baby. From the expression on her face, it could have been either Paul Newman or the Abominable Snowman.

A sudden silence fell on the patio. Several of the other guests had obviously caught sight of this vision too. Baby turned around. Sweets and Martine, arm in arm, were just approaching the hostess booth.

'You know what, Robin?' said Baby. 'This is a historic moment – and we're here to witness it.'

'I guess you're right,' said Robin in what for her were hushed tones. 'If you think about it, next to the day I met Danny and the day the braces came off my teeth, this is probably the most important day of my life.'

They watched as the hostess led Sweets and Martine to a place in the center of the patio. Just about everyone else on the terrace watched too. Especially Carl Terhune, the anniversary man from Chicago, who was sitting at the next table with his wife.

Sweets nodded a greeting to Carl, but Carl, apparently not as friendly when he was sober as when he was drunk, just glared back.

'How quick they forget,' Sweets whispered to Martine. 'The other night I was the best piano player since Art Tatum.' He gave her a reassuring smile. 'Or at least Liberace.'

But Carl, when at last he spoke, didn't whisper. 'What's the matter, honey?' he screamed at Paulette. 'Is this upsetting you?'

Paulette, who had been too involved in trying to figure out what the secret ingredient in her potato salad was to notice what was going on, looked up quickly. 'What, Carl?'

Carl decided that what she'd said was 'yes'. In a voice now loud enough to be heard over by the pool, he said to Paulette, 'I'm going to ask for another table. We're payin' good money to be here, we don't have to put up with this.'

Paulette leaned across the table. 'Is there something wrong, dear?' she asked in her quiet, hesitant way. In the twenty years she'd been married to Carl not a day had gone by when there hadn't been something wrong.

Carl ignored her. In the twenty years they'd been married not a day had gone by when he hadn't ignored her. He snapped his fingers at the hostess. 'Oh, Miss!' he called. 'Miss! My wife and I would like a table away from the riff-raff.'

The hostess froze in place, still smiling like a Barbie Doll.

Robin and Baby looked at one another. 'Uh oh,' muttered Baby. 'I wonder where my dad is.'

Robin shifted in her seat uneasily. 'When you said historic moment I didn't know you had Pearl Harbor in mind,' she mumbled.

'It's all that Kennedy's fault!' Carl boomed, in case there was anyone in a ten-mile radius who was interested in hearing this information. 'Fillin' their heads up with all that crap . . .'

Sweets was concentrating on reading the specials of the day, but he was getting visibly tenser and tenser. If he held the menu any tighter it was going to snap in two.

Paulette looked puzzled. 'What's Kennedy's fault, dear?' she asked patiently. Then her face brightened. 'You mean because he's a Catholic?'

Martine leaned towards Sweets. 'Maybe we should come back later,' she suggested. 'After the windbag's gone.'

'Uh uh,' said Sweets between clenched teeth. 'Not this time, babe. Everybody's been looking at us like we had eight heads between us. We're staying right here.' He took her hand in his but his eyes went to Carl. 'This is the future,' he said in a clear, strong voice, 'and certain people just better get used to it.'

'Bravo!' said Baby, only half under her breath.

Robin kicked her under the table. 'Baby, for Pete's sake,' she hissed, 'what are you trying to do, start a race riot?'

But several of the other guests nodded their silent agreement.

'I don't have to get used to nothing,' growled Carl, suddenly standing over Sweets and Martine.

Paulette reached over and grabbed his arm. 'Why don't you sit down and finish your lunch, dear?' she asked nervously. 'You know you've got that ul—'

He shook her off as though she were a fly. 'My future does not include the likes of you two,' he roared. 'No, sirree, Bob. I didn't fight the war so you two could flaunt yourselves in my face.'

'Maybe you were fightin' on the wrong side then,' said a cool voice behind him.

Carl turned to find Johnny standing there, looking him straight in the eyes. 'You just mind your own business, boy.' He pointed to Sweets. 'It's *him* I've got the gripe with. Him and that white trash.' He swung back to Sweets. 'I want you and her outta here, and I want you out now.'

'We're not goin' anywhere, Mr Terhune,' said Sweets evenly. 'Not now, not ever.'

Carl took a step forward. 'Well, maybe you just need an escort, nigger.' Before anyone could move he'd grabbed Sweets by the front of his shirt and was pulling him to his feet.

Just as quickly, Johnny lunged forward and knocked Carl to the ground. 'That's it,' he said quietly, pulling himself off the older man. 'It's all over.'

Carl dusted himself off. 'Sure thing,' he said, getting to his feet. 'You're the boss.'

By now all the other diners on the patio were on their feet as well. There was an audible sigh of relief as Carl extended his hand to Johnny.

'No hard feelins', huh?' said Carl. 'I guess I just get a little carried away with myself sometimes.'

Johnny made a move to shake – and in that second Carl punched him hard and he fell to the ground with a loud gasp.

'Johnny!'

Carl turned to Sweets. 'Now it's your turn, nigger,' he smiled. But before he could land a punch, Sweets had wiped the smile from his face with a punch of his own, a solid right hook that sent him reeling.

'You wouldn't call Cassius Clay a nigger to his face,' Sweets said quietly to the recumbent figure, whose head was resting on a chair rung, 'and you'd better *never* do it to me again neither!'

Seven

'I hope you're happy now,' Johnny grumbled. 'You've got your dragons and your knights in shining armor . . . you and your freakin' fairy tales. You must be over the moon.'

'Hold still, will you?' Baby was trying to put some iodine on the bruise on Johnny's face, but he kept moving away. 'I don't know what you're talking about. That was more like *Gunfight at the O.K. Corral* than *Snow White*.'

'Ouch! Watch it, will ya? You're gonna get that junk in my eye.'

'I'm nowhere near your eye. If you'd just stop moving around . . .'

He pushed her hand away. 'I'm all right, I tell you. Stop makin' such a fuss.'

She held the dropper poised. 'But if you don't put something on it it could get infected. My mother always says that—'

'Frances, I don't care what your mother always says. I bet she always made you take your multivitamin capsules every morning and brush your hair a hundred times before you went to bed, too.'

Baby blushed.

'I knew it!' cried Johnny. He started to laugh but ended up wincing in pain. 'I bet you still—'

'We're not concerned about me right now,' said Baby, recovering herself. How could he possibly know she took vitamins before breakfast and how many times she brushed her hair at night? 'We're concerned with you.'

'Do you eat something from all the major food groups every day too?'

'Johnny, that's really a nasty—'

'Forget it, will ya? I'd certainly like to. Imagine lettin' a jerk like that sucker punch you. I had worse fights than that when I was in grade school.' He got to his feet. 'If you wanna do somethin' constructive, why don't you help Sherry clean up the mess?'

Now that she wasn't actually looking at him she could ask what she'd wanted to ask from the start. 'How come you did it, Johnny?'

'How come I did what?'

Why was it never possible to ask him a straight question and get a straight answer in return? 'How come you let that jerk sucker punch you?' she wisecracked. And then, turning towards him, 'How come you got involved?'

Sometimes he didn't know if he wanted to shake her or hug her. Now she was going to give him this big thank-you speech for acting like some stupid storybook hero, and it hadn't even occurred to her that he'd be lucky if he didn't lose his job for this. That instead of doing something to be proud of he'd acted just like the dumb hood her father always accused him of being. Attacking a Kellerman guest. Geez, he should have his head examined. If only he could convince himself that this was all her fault. Her and her stupid romantic notions. At least then he'd have someone else to blame, even if Max didn't. But it wasn't Baby who'd made him throw himself on top of Chicago's answer to Adolf Hitler. He'd done that all by himself. ' 'Cause your old man's right, that's why. Guys like me, we don't know how to think, so we just start punchin'.'

Baby looked at the iodine bottle. Maybe what was so fascinating about Johnny was the fact that no matter what she said to him she was always wrong. If she said something critical of him she was wrong because she didn't understand him or where he came from. If she tried to praise him he'd scream. Baby sighed. 'That's not true, Johnny. What you did was really brave. Standing up like that . . .' It was amazing how much information they could put on one little bottle. But at least reading the application instructions for iodine was safer than saying anything more. There was certainly no way she could tell him how proud she was of the way he'd behaved. That there wasn't another guy she knew who would have put himself forward like that. Especially not when it might cost him his job. And there was certainly no way she could tell him how her heart had stopped beating for a second when she heard Carl Terhune's fist slam into him. She raised her eyes to his. 'And I thought you didn't believe in—'

Here it came. She thought he didn't believe in true love. She thought he didn't think love was more important than where you came from or where you went to school or what sorts of presents your parents gave you for your birthday when you were a kid. Boy, did he wish she wouldn't look at him like that. 'Don't tell me what I do and don't believe in, OK, Baby?' he shouted, turning on his heel. ' 'Cause you don't know.'

* * *

Everyone has a different way of relaxing after a day of stress and pressure. In the days when he worked in an office, Max used to unwind by mowing the lawn. Robin's father had a model railroad where he'd spend hours watching the Speedball Express chug around the track, calling out the stops and pretending to be the whistle. Johnny's father liked to unwind by playing darts. President Kennedy played touch football. Johnny and Sweets, both on edge since the fight, had run into each other on the way to the basketball court.

The ball flew over Sweets' head, hovered on the rim for a split second, then fell through the basket.

Johnny gave out a war-whoop of victory, ignoring the pain that moving his facial muscles caused him. 'I told ya, man. It's one of nature's rules. The earth revolves around the sun. Leaves fall off the trees in the autumn. And all the best basketball players come from Jersey. You don't stand a chance against me.'

Sweets strolled across the court, dribbling the ball with his bandaged hand. 'It's because I've got three inches of gauze wrapped around my knuckles that you're scorin' all the baskets, Castle,' he laughed. 'And don't you forget it.' He pivoted around, heading back towards the basket, picking up speed, but Johnny leapt up and blocked the shot at the last minute. 'And because I'm an old man,' panted Sweets, throwing himself on the ground. 'Let's not forget that either.'

'You're not old,' grinned Johnny, collapsing beside him. 'You just can't play basketball for beans.'

Sweets looked down at his injured hand. 'I'm too old for some things, though, Johnno, I'll tell you that.'

'You mean Mr Terhune?'

'I mean bar brawlin'. I thought I'd left that sort of thing behind me a long time ago.'

Johnny threw a pebble across the court. 'I'm sorry about that, Sweets, that was all my fault. I don't know what got into me.'

Sweets picked up a few pebbles of his own, weighing them in his hand. 'It wasn't your fault, Johnny. Something like that was bound to happen. The man gives baboons a bad name.'

Johnny threw another stone across the asphalt. 'Yeah, maybe. I dunno. How's Martine takin' it?'

'About how you'd expect. She didn't grow up thinkin' she might have a fight on her hands every time she stepped out of the house.' He let the pebbles fall from his hand. 'Anyway, I wanted to thank you for steppin' in like that.'

Johnny looked at him in surprise. 'Thank me?'

'Yeah, thank you. I wish none of it had happened, but I think you did the right thing.' He stared into the distance. 'And I appreciate the support. I'm not used to havin' someone on my team like that.'

Johnny shrugged him off. 'Yeah. Well, I bet Max doesn't think I did the right thing.'

Sweets pointed across the court, to where Norman was hurrying towards them, waving in agitation. 'I think we're about to find out.'

Max's office had been designed not just as a place of work, but as a place where he could retreat from the pressures and problems of his busy day. The walls were a calming blue. The carpet was a tranquil gray. The shades were adjusted so just enough pleasant sunshine filtered through. Pictures of peaceful pastoral scenes decorated the walls. About the only thing in Max's office at the moment that wasn't calm, tranquil, pleasant or peaceful was Max himself. He was standing behind his desk, unheedful of the advice the doctor had given him about his blood pressure, pointing an angry finger at Johnny.

'You!' he was shouting. 'I hold you completely responsible for all this! Completely! I knew the minute I clapped eyes on you that you'd be nothing but trouble, and nothing but trouble is exactly what you have been. Always giving everybody lip, never knowing your place, always so smooth and charming when you want—'

'Me?' Johnny shouted back. 'What the heck did I do? Oh don't tell me, don't tell me,' waving his hands in the air. 'The guest is never wrong, right? Kellerman Commandment Numero Uno. The guest can insult people and bully everyone and act like he's Hitler and everybody else is Poland, but that's OK. He's *always* right.'

'No,' roared Max. 'I mean, that is the rule . . . that's what I said, but no, that's not OK. However, that doesn't excuse you assaulting—'

Johnny rested his hands on the edge of the desk. 'The guest can be built like a freakin' Mack truck, but if a person tries to even up the odds a little, he's right away a criminal.'

'Never mind evening up the odds!' Max was turning a rather remarkable shade of red. He leaned towards Johnny. 'You should have stopped the fight!'

'I was tryin' t'stop the fight,' screamed Johnny. 'What'd you think I was tryin' t'do?'

'Well, you didn't do a very good job, did you? Because instead of breaking up the fight you broke Mr Terhune's nose.'

All during this exchange, Sweets had been standing next to Johnny, waiting for a chance to say something. His chance had come. 'Actually,' he said, loudly but calmly, 'I was the one who broke Mr Terhune's nose.'

'I woulda broken his head if I'd had the chance,' yelled Johnny. 'I don't care whose guest he is!'

Max looked from one to the other. 'What?'

'I broke his nose,' repeated Sweets.

'But I would of if I'd had the chance,' put in Johnny.

Max looked as though he were the one who'd been hit. He stared at Sweets. '*You* broke it?'

Sweets nodded. 'Yeah, I broke it. Look, Max, I'm really sorry about all this, but none of it was Johnny's fault. If it hadn't been for him God knows what would've happened. You should be thanking him, not layin' into him. He only tried to do what you would've done if you'd been there.'

With a thud Max sat down in his chair. 'I can't believe the week I'm having. Guests leaving. One of the most reasonable men I know getting into a punch-up. Now I'm looking at insurance, maybe even a lawsuit . . . Johnny Castle standing up for truth, justice and the American way . . .' He shook his head. 'I just can't believe it. This is worse than Elizabeth selling the house without telling me. This is even worse than discovering I was going bald. I don't think I can take it all in.'

Now it was Sweets' turn to lean on the desk. 'Look, Max, the way people react to me and Martine is our problem. If we're gonna get married, then that's something we've got to face. But you don't. We have no right to drag you into it . . . cause you hassles. Martine and I've gotta go through this together, Max, but if you'd rather we did it someplace else . . .'

Johnny, trying to blend into the walls during this exchange, expected Max to tell both him and Sweets to go – if not to hell then at least to another resort. The Sheldrake, maybe. See if they couldn't lose them business. But to his surprise Max said no such thing.

'Are you crazy?' Max asked, shaking his head. 'There's no way you're going anywhere else. We've got a contract. And, anyway, I sort of like having you in one piece. At least if you're here we can protect you a bit.' He smiled at the pen set on his desk, feeling a little embarrassed for some reason. 'Or you can protect Superman here a bit. Whatever. You're staying right where you are.' With some difficulty, he glanced up at Johnny. 'And that goes for you too', he mumbled.

For one of the few times in his life, Johnny was speechless. He unclenched his hands, only then realizing how tense he had been. Maybe he had been wrong about Max after all. Well, not wrong, but not one hundred per cent right either. Maybe he was guilty of doing what he always accused Max of doing, only looking at the surface. Maybe not all of Baby's spunk and fight came from her mother.

Sweets, too, was at a temporary loss for words. He studied Max for a second. The two of them had been together for a long time, but somehow the important things never seemed to get said. Now, he figured, was as good a time as any. 'You know, Max, some of my friends, they think I'm nuts comin' back here every summer. I could get ten times what you pay me tourin' Europe. Plus the food is better,' he joked. But there was no joke in his voice when he went on. 'I tell them I come back because it's nice to have my toothbrush in the same rack every night for a few months. But it's a lot more than that, y'know. This place is . . . well I guess this place is like my home.' He looked from Max to Johnny. 'And you guys are like my family.'

'Be careful what you're saying, Sweets,' warned Max, trying to sound like he was joking. 'If we're your family then Johnny and I must be related.'

'I've heard of worse things,' laughed Sweets.

'I haven't,' muttered Max.

Johnny, his hand on the doorknob, didn't say a thing.

'OK, I'm here!' called Penny, sauntering into the rehearsal studio. Johnny was over by the record player, his back to her, sorting through the discs. 'Let's see what great new additions you've made to the routine today.' She threw herself into a chair and kicked off her street shoes. 'I just hope Jack Benny appreciates all this. I'd much rather be dipping my toes in the lake than learning new steps right now.'

Johnny put a record on the machine. 'OK,' he said, turning around for the first time, 'I'll go through it first to show you how—'

Penny looked up, and froze with her hand on her dance bag. 'What the heck happened to you? You join the first street gang in the Catskills or somethin'?'

'I ran into somethin', that's all. Now I want you t'pay attention. These steps aren't as easy as they look.'

Penny's eyebrow went up. 'Ran into what?'

'What's it matter?' Johnny turned back to the record player. 'A door, a wall . . . it's no big deal.'

Penny came up beside him, peeking around his shoulder. 'It doesn't looks so good. Did y'put somethin' on it?'

'Yeah, yeah, I put somethin' on it.'

'So who hit you?'

'Look, could we just get some work done here? I told ya. I ran into a wall. This nosey chick was botherin' me an—'

'Hey, Castle, it's me, Penny. The girl with three brothers? The girl who had a bald patch the size of a dime once cause she and Susan O'Malley had a fight in the locker room over some dumb Irish guy. Who hit you?'

Johnny kept his eyes on the record, silently going round and round. 'One of the guests.'

Penny collapsed against him, hooting with laughter. 'One of the guests! One of the guests hit *you*?'

'I'm glad you think it's so funny.'

'Whose husband? Or do y'want me t'guess?' She frowned as though thinking hard. 'Now let's see . . . there's Mrs—'

'Nobody's husband, Miss Wiseguy. It wasn't like that.'

It was rare that anything really surprised Penny, but she looked genuinely surprised now. 'It wasn't a jealous husband? Then who was it?'

Johnny dropped the arm of the record player. 'Come on, let's get started with this or we'll be here all night.'

But Penny was eyeing him shrewdly. 'Wait a minute. It wasn't somethin' t'do with Sweets and his girlfriend, was it?'

He gave her a little shove. 'Go sit down so you can—'

'It was, wasn't it?' She whistled. 'Wow. You got into a fight—'

'It wasn't a fight. It was stopped before it became a fight. Will you go sit down, Penny? I'm in no mood for this.'

'For God's sake, Johnny. I'm concerned. Does Max know?'

'Yeah, Max knows. Halfa Kellerman's knows by now. I'm surprised you didn't know.'

Penny laughed. 'Me? I've been teachin' the under-eights the bunny hop all afternoon. It's like being in the French Foreign Legion only you don't get a uniform.' Her expression became serious. 'So what happened?'

'Nothin' happened. He laid a lucky punch on me and that was it.'

'I meant with Cranky Kellerman. You in trouble?'

'Nope. But I don't know how understanding he'll be if it happens again.'

'And will it?'

'What d'ya mean, "will it?" How do I know? I didn't start it—'

'Yeah, maybe you didn't start it, but you were obviously willin' to finish it.' She bit her lip. 'Oh, Johnny. What if you'd lost your job? What woulda happened then? What woulda happened to me? I just don't know what's gotten into you. You used to be so sensible about . . . about things.'

There was something in the way she was looking at him that reminded him of his mother. It was hard to imagine Penny Lopez, dark and slim and beautiful, being able to remind him of his short, dumpy, round-faced mother, but this was clearly one of those days. She was looking at him just the way his mother looked at him after he'd been arguing with his father. Like there was something important he just didn't understand. 'You weren't there, Pen. You don't know what—'

'No, I wasn't there.' A new suspicion hurried into her brain, at about the same time that the concern hurried out of her voice. 'But I bet Miss Frances Joan of Arc Kellerman was there. Wasn't she?' All at once she wished he'd been *really* hurt, not just scratched up a little. It would have served him right if he'd had both his legs broken. She turned away from him. Suddenly she felt that she might cry. It was definitely time to go. 'And I also know that it wasn't any of your business.'

'Sweets is a friend, Penny. Maybe that makes it my business.'

She thumped across the hall. 'Yeah, well both you and your friend are old enough and smart enough t'know that life is tough enough as it is,' she shouted, putting her shoes back on. 'Y'don't hafta to go out of your way t'look for grief.'

'Meaning?' He started after her as she headed for the door. 'Meaning?'

If she could just stay mad enough till she got out the door, she could keep back the tears. 'Meaning that people should stick to their own kind, that's what!'

The door banged behind her. Johnny stood in the center of the dance floor, staring at the place where she had been. Hearing her voice still screaming in his head.

Stick with your own kind . . . your own kind . . . your own kind . . .

Eight

Martine Jellico was used to being in the public eye, and she was used to dealing with people. You can't get up in front of a classroom full of students without realizing that most of them are probably more interested in what you're wearing and whether or not you have a hangover than they are in Jane Austen. You can't run a successful book store in as eccentric a neighborhood as Greenwich Village without becoming skilled at dealing with difficult types.

But being in the public eye and dealing with people at Bennington and in the Village were not the same as being in the public eye and dealing with people at Kellerman's.

Martine was sitting at a corner table with Robin and Baby, trying to look interested in what Robin was saying about how many sets of tennis you had to play to work off a three-inch slice of chocolate cheesecake, but her mind was on the fact that every time she looked up some new pair of eyes was staring at her. Training as a Green Beret probably couldn't have prepared her for Kellerman's, she thought ruefully.

'I don't understand why you're so obsessed with your weight,' Baby said. 'You'd never catch me scraping the chocolate off the chocolate graham crackers. I just eat whatever I like and I never gain an ounce.'

Robin made a face. 'Oh, God,' she sighed. 'It's like trying to explain to Jackie Kennedy what it's like to be poor. The fact is, Frances Kellerman, that if I wasn't obsessed with my weight I'd look like Moby Dick by now. A handful of chopped nuts and a maraschino cherry on top of my sundae can mean the difference between life and death for my hips.'

'What I can't understand,' said Martine, trying not to notice that the couple at the next table was pointing at her, 'is why everyone here is so obsessed with me.' Everywhere she went heads turned. If she walked into a room all conversation immediately stopped. If she went into the shop for a newspaper or a candy bar, or if she stopped someone to ask them the time, they would gawp at her as though they couldn't believe she knew how to talk. No matter where she went – for a stroll across the golf course or for a swim in the pool – there was always someone watching her, talking about her. 'That's her!' she'd hear them say. 'No! Really? Well, I'll be!'

Baby smiled sympathetically. 'I'm sure it'll settle down. You know, now that the Terhunes have gone . . .'

'Yeah,' agreed Robin, 'everybody just has to get used to the idea.'

'Robin,' said Martine, 'this country is nearly two hundred years old and no one's gotten used to the idea yet.'

Baby's eyes went from Martine to the ice cube melting in the drink in front of her. 'Maybe it's you that'll have to get used to them,' she suggested quietly. 'You know . . . learn to ignore them.'

Martine's lips made a movement, but it was hard to call it a smile. 'Yeah, well . . .' Martine looked over to where Sweets was playing with the band. Just seeing him strengthened her resolve. Just seeing him reminded her how right they were – right for each other and right to want to be together. But when she was on her own . . . Somehow, she'd really thought that this time it would be different. That this time the looks and the whispers and the hostile comments wouldn't get to her. But instead it was just the same. Instead, when she was by herself she felt like all she wanted to do was run away and hide. And that fight. Sweets had never actually come to blows with anyone before. She was beginning to know what it must be like to be a deer in the Maine woods on the first day of the hunting season. Vulnerable. Endangered. Unlikely to make it to nightfall without someone taking a shot at you. The band started playing 'Moonglow'. Her eyes met Sweets', just for a heartbeat. 'Yeah,' said Martine, smiling for real. 'I guess I'll just have to get used to it.'

Kellerman's was more a day-time than a night-time sort of place. Of course, there were always one or two guests who liked to keep the bartender company until the early hours of the morning, a few summer lovers who found it hard to say good night, and the movable gin game. But after a heavy day of popsicle stick sculpting, badminton, golf and potato-sack races, most of Kellerman's liked to get to bed at an early hour. Sweets, who had spent most of his adult life going home at dawn, found this convenient. It meant that on nights like tonight, when he couldn't sleep and needed to think, he could sit at the piano in the ballroom for as long as he liked, playing the blues.

He looked out at the now empty room. It was a relief just to have gotten through the evening, knowing that everyone was talking about him, watching him, craning their necks to see if they could catch a glimpse of Martine. Sweets started fooling around with 'Heart and Soul'. He'd been a little surprised that Martine had actually joined the fun-loving families of Kellerman's in the ballroom tonight, since she'd been lying low most of the afternoon. He had the feeling that the fight had gotten to her even more than he'd thought – the fight and all the attention – but he was in such a state of turmoil himself that he was almost afraid to ask. He was just going to have to trust that this time when she said she could handle it she really could. At least this time she had Baby and Robin standing by her. The three of them had left together before the last set.

'Why don't you play that song like you mean it?'

Sweets turned. There she was, standing at the stage entrance, looking like she'd just stepped out of heaven.

'Martine!' Instead of picking up the tempo, he came to a dead stop.

She came over to the piano, sliding onto the bench beside him. 'I thought I might find you still here, noodling away, just like old times.' She picked out a few notes with one finger. 'I just wanted to let you know that I'm not giving up.'

He laid his hand on hers. 'Did I say you were?'

Her head rested on his shoulder. 'No. But you were thinking it.'

'And what about you? Why'd you leave before the show was over?'

She started reaching into her pocket. 'I wanted to go make a list.'

'A list?' he laughed. 'You're goin' shoppin' in the mountains in the middle of the night?'

'No, silly. I made a list of the things that frighten me the most.' She took a small sheets of white paper out and opened it.

'Let me see,' he said, grabbing at it.

'Oh no you don't, don't look. I'll read it to you.' She cleared her throat. 'One. Children.'

'Now that's a good one,' said Sweets. 'I was wonderin' when we were gonna get around to talkin' about them again. You worried that they'll come out lookin' like their mama or their daddy?'

'I did give it a lot of thought. I mean, you're not the most beautiful man the world has ever seen . . . that nose, for instance . . .'

'Come on, babe, this isn't funny, it's serious. Too serious to be joked about.'

'No, Sweets, it's too serious not to be joked about. We're not going to get anywhere if we don't maintain our sense of humor. Anyway, what I decided was that all kids have their crosses to bear. I had my big feet. You had that nose . . .'

'Martine—'

'As long as we love each other and we love our kids, they'll get through it. That's all anybody can do.'

He looked at her thoughtfully. The last time they'd broken up kids had been one of the major reasons. Then she'd said she couldn't put innocent children through so much hassle. 'You're sure about that?'

'Positive.'

'What's number two?'

'Fights.'

He laughed grudgingly. 'Fights are probably numbers two, three, four, five, six and seven.'

'No, just two.'

His expression became serious. 'It'll happen again, you know. No matter how hard I try to stop it, somewhere, some time . . .'

'Then I suggest you get in training. At the very least you'd better insure your fingers.'

'Look, babe, I saw your face after that fight with Terhune. You kept away for hours . . . you—'

She stopped him with a kiss. 'It's like Baby says, honey. There are just some things I'm going to have to learn to ignore. The sight of you throwing men built like football players into the crockery is obviously one of them. You'll just have to try not to do it too often. Because now we're coming to the most important thing of all. Number three.'

'Number three, huh? And what's that? Being investigated by the FBI for being married to someone who belongs to CORE?'

'No,' said Martine. 'Number three of the things I'm most afraid of is losing you.'

It might have been the heat, or the anticipation of having Jack Benny come up on the weekend, or it might have been something else, but tonight seemed to be a night of restlessness. People who were normally tucked up in their cabins, putting pink goo on their faces or brushing their hair a hundred times, were out walking in the moonlight instead. People who were normally dancing the night away in the arms of fiery young women with jealous streaks were out by themselves, walking in the moonlight too. Johnny ran into Robin and Baby by the old wooden footbridge.

Instead of greeting them as one midnight walker to another, he snapped their heads off. 'What are you two doin' out here by yourselves? Don't you know the woods can be dangerous? What if you ran into a bear?'

Baby started to walk by. She was still smarting from the argument they'd had when she was trying to give him first aid. Was there ever a time, she wondered, when she wasn't annoyed with him about something? 'Well we didn't run into a bear, did we? We ran into a wolf instead.'

Robin, wondering what that whirring noise in the bushes was, tittered nervously.

'Ha ha,' laughed Johnny. 'If Bob Hope ever retires you could get a job entertainin' the troops.'

'And just what are you doing out here all by yourself? Don't you know the woods can be dangerous?'

'I had some things I wanted to think about.'

'Think?' laughed Baby. '*You* think? I thought all you did was start punchin'.'

'Well,' said Robin brightly, wondering if she should try to step between them, 'now that we've all found each other, maybe we should go back together.' Marching around in the dark with things going click and crunch and chipchipchip behind her was not Robin's idea of a fun evening. She'd only agreed to come out and risk possible death at the hands of killer bats because she knew Max would murder her if he found out she'd let Baby go off on her own. After all, part of her reason for living here this summer was to keep Baby company and to keep her out of trouble.

'Robin,' said Baby in her most threatening voice, 'we are perfectly capable of getting back on our own.'

'That's a great idea,' said Johnny, taking each of them by an elbow. 'We can stop by the machine and get a Coke.'

Robin decided not to think about the fact that walking around in the night and drinking Cokes with Johnny might not be Uncle Max's idea of keeping Baby out of trouble.

'That's funny,' said Johnny as they came out into the area of the staff quarters, 'it almost looks like the door to Sweets' cabin is open.'

The three of them came to a halt.

Robin squinted into the darkness. 'Nah,' she said, with some relief, 'I think it's just a shadow.'

But Baby was shaking her head. 'I think Johnny's right. It looks like it's wide open, only there isn't any light on inside or anything.'

Johnny let go of them. 'Look, you two stay here. I'll just go take a quick look.'

'Oh no you don't,' said Baby, right behind him, Robin in tow. 'You wanted us with you and that's where we're staying.'

'All right, all right. But be quiet, will ya? We don't know—'

'You mean there might be someone in there?' gasped Robin. 'But what if—'

Baby yanked her forward. 'Robin,' she hissed, 'for once in your life, stop talking.'

As stealthily as they could, given the darkness and the fact that Robin insisted on holding on to both Johnny and Baby – and given the fact that Robin did find it incredibly difficult to stop talking completely – they approached Sweets' room.

'Oh my God,' gasped Robin.

As Johnny had thought, the door was wide open – but it hadn't been opened with a key.

'Do you think they're still in there?' whispered Baby.

Johnny shook his head. 'I'll go in first. You be ready to go for help.'

Holding his breath, he went up to the door. The room inside was completely quiet. He couldn't even hear the ticking of a clock. He took a step into the room, half-expecting to be jumped or dragged inside suddenly. Nothing. He took another step. Was that something moving in the corner? Was that a sound coming from the bathroom? He eased forward, waiting for his eyes to get accustomed to the dark. And then, just when he was least expecting it, a sudden hand on his shoulder made him jump.

'Why don't you turn on the light?' asked Baby behind him.

He swung around on her, forgetting they were supposed to be talking in whispers. 'For the love a Mike, Frances Kellerman. What are y'tryin' t'do? Make my children orphans? Don't ever sneak up on me like that—'

'Here it is!' cried Robin, locating the switch.

The lights went on.

There were three sharp intakes of breath.

'What the heck . . .' breathed Johnny, his eyes taking in the scene before him but his brain having difficulty making any sense of it.

Baby was wide-eyed with horror. 'Who would do something like this?'

And for the first time in her life, Robin Kellerman was completely speechless.

The room was a total shambles. Every surface had been cleared. The closet and the dresser and the desk had been emptied. Clothes, books and photographs had been ripped up and scattered all over. The curtains had been pulled from the windows, the sheets had been pulled from the bed, the mattress had been slashed at least a dozen times.

'I don't believe this,' Robin said, finally finding her voice, 'it's like something out of *Dragnet*.'

'This couldn't happen here,' protested Baby, her voice wobbling. 'Not at Kellerman's . . .'

'Well, it has happened here,' said Johnny, pulling himself together with a certain amount of effort. 'Look, you two stay here. I'll go find Sweets. He has t'be told about this right away.'

'Told about what?' asked Sweets, coming up behind them with Martine.

The three of them stepped out of the doorway. 'Told about this,' said Johnny, pointing into the room.

Nine

Johnny, Baby and Robin were sitting on the steps of the girls' bungalow, each of them staring silently out into the darkness, lost in their own thoughts. It was the same night it had been – the night the special on the dinner menu was salmon, the night Robin was scheduled to shave her legs, the night Norman ended the entertainment in the ballroom with his routine about going to the World's Fair with his parents – but in a matter of minutes it had become a different world.

'Well,' said Baby, her voice sounding unusually loud in the quiet, 'so much for everybody loving a lover.'

It was freakin' fantastic how quickly things could change, Johnny was thinking to himself. You thought everything was settled, predictable, that you knew what was what, and all of a sudden, bamwhamfazam. He watched a star fall out of the sky. How many summers had he been coming up to Kellerman's? Enough that he thought he knew the place inside and out. It was an ordinary place where ordinary well-off people came with their families for a few weeks of cold bortsch and badminton. The people who came up here were maybe not the most exciting people you could hope to meet, they certainly weren't the avant-garde, but they were nice enough. They were just regular people, the sort you would find anywhere. They worried about their kids and their taxes and whether or not they should have the house weather stripped. They fought about which of them was the worse driver. They gave to charities and carried around pictures of their pets. If there was a Western showing in the resort movie theatre, they always rooted for the good guys.

And now this. A punch-up in the heat of the moment was one thing, but deliberately ransacking someone's room, destroying all his possessions . . . what sort of person did something like that?

'It's really weird isn't it?' asked Robin, almost as though she were reading his thoughts. 'It's like finding out that Ozzie and Harriet work for the Mafia. All this time you've been watching him schlumping around in that old sweater and you thought the worse thing he'd ever done in his life was maybe double-park while he went in the store to get a new toothbrush, and then you discover that he's really a hit man.'

'I know what you mean,' said Baby. 'If anybody'd told me even a week ago that something like this could happen at Kellerman's I'd've said they were crazy. Family arguments, kids who puke in the dining room because their mother insists they eat liver, fights over golf scores . . . but doing somebody's room over . . .' She hit her foot against the step. 'I guess you were right all along, Johnny. I never really thought about what Sweets and Martine were up against. Not really. What it must be like to be him . . .' She turned to the young man sitting next to her, looking down at his hands, deep in his own thoughts. 'Or what it must be like to be y— well, to be different . . .'

What was it she'd said about ordinary people changing things? If ordinary people could act like this, could keep so much hatred going, then maybe she was right – they were also the only ones who could ever make things different. You had to change things bit by bit, in your own life. It was fear that held people back – being afraid to do what you knew was right. And if you could lose hold of reality so quickly, maybe she was right again that you had to grab hold of what you wanted – what you believed in, what you loved – when you had the chance. Because what else was there? What else could you count on?

'Johnny? Did you hear me?' She gave him a nudge. 'I was sort of apologizing.'

He met her eyes. 'What for? You're not gonna tell me it was you turned Sweets' place over?'

'No, of course not. I—'

'Then there's no problem, is there?' He got to his feet. 'Look, you guys, I'm really beat. I'll see ya tomorrow, OK?'

Now what had gotten into him? It was absolutely true. No matter what she said to him it was the wrong thing. 'Yeah, sure,' said Baby, 'we'll see you tomorrow.'

'So what do you think?' asked Robin as Baby's eyes watched Johnny disappear into the night.

'About what?'

'About Sweets and Martine. What do you think they're going to do?'

Baby rested her chin on her hands. 'Don't ask me,' she said with a sigh. 'I no longer feel confident in my ability to predict human behavior.'

'Baby,' said Robin. 'Does this mean you're not going to join the Peace Corps after all?'

Martine was bustling around the small room like a manic housekeeper. She'd put the curtains back up, she'd remade the bed, slashed mattress included, and now she was frantically straightening out everything that could be straightened out and putting everything that couldn't be salvaged into a cardboard box. Sweets sat on the bed, just watching as she flitted from the desk to the closet to the bureau, putting things back as though her life depended on it.

She stopped for a second in the middle of the room, holding up a picture. 'You have a hammer?'

'A hammer? Babe, if I had a hammer they probably would've thrown it through the window. What do you want a hammer for?'

She tapped her foot nervously, her bracelets jangling. 'So I can hang this picture back up on the wall.'

'Honey,' said Sweets gently, 'you don't have to do all this tonight. It can wait.'

'No it can't,' said Martine, her voice sounding sharp. 'The sooner everything's back to normal the sooner we can forget that it ever happened.' She looked at the picture in her hand, a photograph of Sweets sitting outside a Parisian café. She had the same picture sitting on her dresser at home. Only the one on her dresser still had glass in the frame. 'Maybe if I use my shoe—'

He got up and took the picture from her hands. 'Look, babe, you've gotta slow down, OK?'

'I can't stop now, Sweets. You know me, Miss Neat and Tidy. It's all my mother's fault. She had plastic over everything – the couch, the table, the carpet . . .'

'Martine, this has nothin' to do with winning the good housekeeping award, and you know it. And you also know that just patchin' everything back together isn't going to make tonight go away.'

She snatched the picture back. 'Yes, it will.'

'Honey, look at me.'

Her voice wavered, but she kept her head bent. 'It's just that every time I close my eyes I see the room the way . . . What if one of us – I can't stand it. I don't want to remember it like that. I—'

He took her in his arms. 'You want to pretend that tonight never happened, Martine, but it did happen.'

She leaned her head against his chest, wrapping her arms around him.

'What if it happens again?'

'It won't.'

'But what if it does?'

She shrugged. 'Then I'll clean up the mess again.'

'And what if it happens again, after that? How many times are you gonna be willin' to clean up the mess? How many times do you think that'll change things?'

She hugged him more tightly.

'Martine . . .' He tilted her face up so that she was looking at him and not his shirt. 'I wanna know what you're thinkin' right now.'

She tried to smile. 'I'm thinking that that's the bad thing about housework. As soon as you do it you have to do it again.'

'Really.'

Her lip trembled as the tears began to fall. 'Oh, Sweets, I don't know what I'm thinking. I'm so confused . . . confused and upset and . . . I don't know, I thought I had everything worked out, I really did . . . I do . . . it's just . . .'

She was crying for real now. Just the way she used to.

'You know what I'm afraid of most, Martine?' He stroked her hair. 'I'm afraid that one day, not tomorrow or the next day, but maybe five years from now, or ten – that one day you're gonna look at me and you're not going to know why you put yourself and your kids through so much garbage. That's what scares me the most. Or that one day I'm gonna look at you and I'm gonna wonder the same thing.'

'But things are changing, Sweets,' she said in a voice choked by tears, 'they really are.' She was pleading, but it was hard to tell whether it was with him or with herself. 'Maybe in ten years nothing like this would ever happen.'

'Maybe it would and maybe it wouldn't. And maybe things are changin', hon', but that doesn't mean that they're changin' fast enough for us. How long do you think I could live with myself, lookin' into your eyes and seein' all the pain I was causing you?'

'But it's not you who's causin'—'

He kissed the top of her head. 'Honey, when it comes down to it, I'd rather be the man you loved and lost than the man you got and used to love.'

Johnny came into the staff room just as Fats Domino began to sing, 'Ain't That a Shame'. He paused in the doorway, listening to the music, watching the one other person in the room, his back to him as he stared into the night.

'Did she get on the train all right?' asked Sweets without turning around.

Johnny came into the room. 'Yeah, she got on the train all right.' He walked over to the window where Sweets was standing, stopping behind him.

'Don't look at me like that,' ordered Sweets.

'Like what?' snapped Johnny. 'You can't even see me.'

'I don't hafta see you to know how you're lookin' at me. I can feel it. You're lookin' at me like I had a clear shot at the basket and I purposely fumbled the ball.'

Johnny moved over to sit on the window ledge, facing Sweets. 'Well, I don't get it, man.'

'Oh yeah? What don't y'get?'

'She just sat there all the way to the station like I was takin' her to the guillotine or somethin'. I get back here and you're lookin' up at the stars playin' heartbreakers on the record player, lookin' like your best friend just got buried. Do you love each other, or what?'

Sweets looked away. 'It's not as simple as you make it sound, Johnno.'

'Yes it is,' said Johnny quietly. 'I used to think it wasn't, but now I know I was wrong.'

'Well, you weren't wrong. You don't know how I feel, or what I've given up, or why. You can't know. You can't get inside this skin, see things with these eyes.'

Johnny leaned towards him, insistent. '*Do you love each other*? It's an easy question.'

'But it's not the only question, Johnny. The other question is: "Is love enough?" And the answer to that is: "Not right now".' He started walking from the room. Just as he reached the doorway he turned back to Johnny. 'Maybe someday the answer will be yes, Johnno. I pray it will be. But right now there are some things that are just bigger and stronger than love.'

Johnny kept his eyes on the spot where Sweets had just been. 'Oh no there aren't,' he said to the empty room. 'You can't let there be.' Outside a breeze stirred the trees. Johnny turned to the night. 'You gotta tell them all to go jump in the lake,' he said in a loud, clear voice. 'Just go jump in the freakin' lake.'

Max came up to where Baby was sitting on the verandah, taking a break from serving the famished masses of Kellerman's their breakfasts. 'Well,' he said, putting an arm around her shoulders, 'if it isn't my favorite waitress. A penny for your thoughts.'

She smiled up at him. 'I was just thinking how peaceful everything seems now. You know, how quickly it all went back to normal.'

'I know,' said Max. 'You wouldn't think that a day or two ago I was thinking of calling in the National Guard, would you?'

Baby sighed. 'Well, at least you must be happy. Nobody's leaving or trying to beat up your staff.'

Max shrugged. 'Yeah, well. I can't say I'm sorry the violence has died down, but I'm a little sad that things didn't work out after all.'

Baby looked at him in surprise. 'You were?'

'Yes, Frances, I was. I know you think of me as a hardhearted and ruthless businessman, but I do have a romantic side to my nature, you know.'

Baby rolled her eyes, thinking of the affair Max had had that had ruined his marriage. 'Oh, yeah, Dad, I know about that.'

'That wasn't what I meant,' said Max, now and then able to read her mind. 'And anyway, I've been thinking a lot about what you said the other day. You know, about the ideals this country is meant to stand for . . . well, you were right. If we don't fight for them they'll be taken from us. I guess I would've been willing to see a few more guests leave Kellerman's if it meant protecting someone's freedom. After all,' said Max, clearing his throat and putting on the voice he used for his most boring staff lectures, 'all men are created equal . . .'

'Wow, Mr Kellerman,' said Norman, suddenly appearing out of thin air to clap him on the shoulder, 'do you really mean that? Do you think you and I are equal?'

'Norman,' said Max, trying to keep his smile friendly, 'you know what I think of you?'

'No, what?'

Max took Norman by the arm and headed him back in the direction from which he had come. 'I think of you as the son I never wanted.'

'Gee, Mr Kellerman,' grinned Norman, 'that's the nicest thing you ever said to me.'

Ten

'But Mr Kellerman,' Norman was saying as he trotted along beside Max. 'You said you'd think about it. Remember? You promised.'

Max smiled as pleasantly as a man whose body seemed to be melting in the heat and who was being harangued by a desperate comic could smile. 'I did think about it, Norman. And the answer is no.'

But all I'm asking is that you introduce me,' Norman pleaded. 'That's all. Just a quick introduction. "Norman, this is Jack Benny. Jack, this is Norman Bryant, one of the most brilliant and original young comedians the Bortsch Belt has ever seen".' Norman mopped the sweat from his brow as they hurried along. Max, checking the list in his hand, didn't so much as glance his way. He tried again. ' "Jack, Norm. Norm, Jack." Is that too much to ask, Mr Kellerman? A simple introduction?'

'Yes,' snapped Max, turning his list into a fan. 'It's too much to ask. In this heat everything is too much to ask.' He reached in his pocket for his own handkerchief. 'I knew I should've had the whole place air-conditioned when Morty Feinberg's brother offered me that great deal last year. But, oh, no, I was too smart. It never gets that hot up here, I told him. It always cools off at night.' He waved his list in Norman's face. 'So now here I am having to buy all these darn fans.'

'You know what we always did at home?' asked Norman, helpful as ever.

Max groaned inwardly. 'No, Norm, what did you always do at home?'

'We put the sheets in the refrigerator.'

Max stopped so quickly that Norman nearly walked right by him. Max raised his eyes to the sky. 'Now, why didn't I think of that?' he asked. He returned his gaze earthwards. 'That would really impress Jack Benny, wouldn't it, Norm? Just a minute, Mr Benny, I'll just get your sheets. We've put them in the refrigerator between the milk and the sour cream.'

'What's wrong with that?' asked Norman, noticing the sarcasm in Max's voice. 'Isn't it kosher?'

This time Max's groan was not inward. 'Get in the car, Norman,' he ordered, opening the door. 'Just get in the car. It is definitely too hot for me and you.'

It was official. The entire Eastern Seaboard was in the grip of a heat wave. The weather man had stuck a sun on the map covering the tri-state area with a sad smile. 'We're having a heat wave,' he'd joked, pretending to wipe the sweat from his brow. 'It isn't surprising! Boy, is that temperature rising!'

Not that anyone at Kellerman's had needed to be told. For days the thermometer outside the door of Max's office had been climbing and climbing while the guests and staff got limper and limper. There was no longer a wait for the tennis courts. The golf course was almost deserted. The horseshoe tournament had been postponed. The only place you could expect to see bows and arrows was on TV. Only the lake and the pool were crowded. The number of people signing on for dancing lessons had increased sharply as well. 'That's because the instructor's so incredibly cool,' claimed Johnny. 'No it's not,' said Baby. 'It's because the studio has air-conditioning.'

The one positive thing the heat seemed to have done was bring people together. Couples who would normally have separated after breakfast – he to play squash, she to play tennis; he to try his skill at shuffle-board, she to do twenty-five jumping jacks on the back lawn – now stayed together. They sat in the shade, reading or doing crosswords. They stretched out side by side at the pool or the lake front. They sat on the patio sipping tall, cool drinks and gazing into one another's eyes. They had picnic lunches packed for them and went for long drives and boat rides to secluded spots. Kellerman's, home of innertube races and organized hikes, had become the home of long, languid days and sensual evenings. Kellerman's, the family resort, had been turned into Kellerman's, the couple's camping grounds. 'If I didn't know better,' Sweets had said, 'I'd think I was on a tropical island.' Max had glared at him. 'No wonder they always talk about Latin lovers,' he'd said sourly, thinking of the mambo and the rhumba and the cha-cha-cha and Johnny Castle's smile. 'At least the Jersey gigolo should be in his element.'

And as for the staff . . . Submarine race watching had become endemic. The dancing in the staff room had become so hot that everyone was joking that the windows were beginning to melt.

Even Norman and the chef, normally too preoccupied to pay much attention to the opposite sex (Norman with improving his one-liners, the chef with perfecting his boiled brisket), had been seen casting amorous glances in certain directions.

'It's disgusting,' Baby was saying to Robin as they collapsed in the shade of an old oak tree, fanning themselves with paper fans. 'Everywhere you go there's some couple smooching in the corner. You'd think we were on the Ark or something.'

Robin gave her a look. 'Ooooh, who gets bad-tempered in the heat?' She blew air down the front of her blouse. 'Anyway, I for one think it's nice. It makes the place seem romantic.' She waved her fan faster. 'Hot, but romantic.' She sighed. 'I only wish Danny were here.'

'There's more to life than having a date, you know,' grumbled Baby. She savagely flicked an ant off her leg. 'Nothing exciting ever happens around here. It's the same thing, day after day. I am *sooo* bored.'

Robin looked at her as though she'd lost her mind. 'Bored? What are you talking about, "bored"? We practically just had a race riot up here. We just watched true love lose to the bad guys. You think that's boring? Your part of Roslyn must be a lot more exciting than mine.'

Baby waved her words away. 'You know what I mean. I thought I was really going to *live* this summer.' The truth was that ever since Martine had gone back home, Baby had been feeling more and more depressed. She had been so caught up with the romance between Sweets and Martine – almost as though it had as much to do with her as with them. She'd believed in them, *really* believed – and then to have it end like that . . . Now she felt as though she was being forced into accepting that Johnny had been right: there were some things love couldn't conquer. There were some obstacles that couldn't be surmounted. But that, unlikely as it seemed, made Neil right: you had to stick to your own kind. And if that were true . . . She threw her fan on the ground. 'But this isn't living.'

'Oh, no?' asked Robin, sarcastically. 'Well, it can't be death because I'm still on a diet.'

'It's waiting,' said Baby flatly. 'It's like starting out on a trip around the world and being held for days at the airport.' She stared across the lawn. In the distance, shimmering in the heat, she could see a couple slowly strolling towards the woods. 'There's this big, wide world outside, just full of adventures and important things to be done, and all anybody around here can think of is what's for lunch and sex.'

Robin snapped her fingers. 'Oh, I know what's getting to you. You're upset because of that moonlight swim business.'

Baby stretched out on her back. 'Moonlight swim?' she repeated, as though she had never heard of either moonlight or swimming. 'Don't be so childish, Robin. I'm upset about life.' Her eyes were focused on a passing cloud. 'Or the lack of it.'

'Oh no, you're not, Frances Kellerman,' said Robin, snapping her fan. 'You were right beside me when Norm said the staff snuck up to that waterfall last night to cool off. Don't pretend you weren't. I saw your face.'

The cloud Baby'd been staring at started to take the shape of a heart. Oh brother, she thought, you can't even look at the sky anymore. 'I don't know what you're talking about, Robin,' she said, shifting her attention to the leaves over their heads. 'Why should I care if a couple of busboys and chambermaids want to go for a swim in the middle of the night?'

'Oh, I'm sure you don't,' said Robin, mimicking Baby's tone. 'But if a couple of dance teachers—'

Baby flopped over on her stomach. 'You're not funny, Robin,' she said shortly. 'I want you to know that.'

Robin gazed up at the heart-shaped cloud. 'Oh, I know,' she said with a smile. 'I know.'

Baby was having a dream. It was hot. She was walking along a tropical beach. Now and then she would pass an amorous couple. The men all wore shorts, the girls all wore grass skirts or sarongs. Baby was dressed in her pink sun dress with the bows on the shoulders, her hair was in a pony tail.

Although it was night, she knew that the sand was white and the turquoise-colored water was as clear as glass. Palm trees swayed. Above her, a giant yellow moon smiled down. She was lost. Well, maybe not lost, but she wasn't where she wanted to be. She knew that. She'd been struggling along the sand for hours. She was trying to escape, though she didn't know from what. She was trying to reach some point just ahead. But no matter how far she walked that point stayed miles and miles away.

Suddenly, she heard music. It was Shelley Fabares. 'Johnny Angel,' Shelley was singing, 'how I love him . . .' She looked around. Shelley

Fabares was sitting in an innertube on the ocean, her sweet voice drifting along on the breeze. And there, at the water's edge, a single couple danced. It was a slow dance. So slow they were almost standing still – but not quite. Baby couldn't see their faces because they were dancing in the cloud of steam that floated up from their bodies. But the couple was familiar. Something about them . . .

She moved a little closer. The girl was wearing skimpy red silk underwear, edged in lace. Her long dark hair swayed as she swayed. Her eyes never moved from her partner's face. His hands never moved from her twisting hips.

Baby started running towards them. 'Let me dance!' she called. The couple didn't miss a beat. 'I want to dance now!' shouted Baby.

She stood beside them. The couple kept staring into each other's eyes. Baby tapped the girl's bare shoulder. 'It's my turn,' she screamed at her. 'It's my turn now.' Shelley Fabares started singing louder. The couple's dancing became more intense. 'Me!' yelled Baby. 'You've had him long enough. It's my turn now!' The girl flung her head back and laughed. Shelley Fabares started laughing. The orchestra that had suddenly popped up in innertubes all around Shelley Fabares started laughing.

'Your turn?' roared the girl. 'You must be kiddin'!"

'Go home, Baby,' shouted Shelley Fabares. 'You don't belong here!'

'Yeah,' the violinists all agreed. 'Go home, Baby! Go back to your own kind!'

Baby grabbed hold of the boy's arm. 'Tell them,' she screamed at him. 'Tell them my name is Frances! Tell them it's my turn! She's had you long enough!' His eyes met hers.

'But, Baby,' he said, 'you can't get across.' He pointed towards her feet. There between them lay an enormous railroad track. Waves broke across the rails. Everyone was laughing. 'You can't get across,' they shouted. 'You can't get across. You have to stay on your side. You have to stay where you belong.'

'My turn!' begged Baby. 'My turn! My turn! My turn . . .'

Baby woke up with a start. The sheet was twisted around her feet, she was drenched in sweat. She looked over at the glowing hands of Robin's alarm clock. It was 2 am. She lay there for a few minutes, breathing heavily, all too aware that not all of the moisture on her face was sweat.

She looked over at Robin, smiling in her sleep. Robin was probably dreaming about Danny. And somewhere out there Danny was probably dreaming about Robin.

Baby sighed. Outside she could hear the night sounds of Kellerman's – the hoot of an owl, the chirping of crickets, the voice of Sam Cooke drifting down from the staff room. There was no way she was going to fall asleep now. 'Drink some warm milk,' said her mother's voice in her head. 'Count sheep,' said Max. 'Count Troy Donahue's teeth,' said Robin. I should go for a walk, Baby said to herself, that's what I should do. She crept from her bed, searching for her clothes in the dark. Cool off.

The night, though thick and hot, was beautiful. Baby looked up at the sparkling stars. She took a deep breath. This is better, she thought. I just needed to get out of that room for a while. Where should she go? To the lake? To the main building? To the pool? To watch the card game that would still be going on in the games room? To the kitchen for something cold to drink? There was a time in the history of the world when all roads were said to lead to Rome. But this was the time in the history of Frances Kellerman when all roads lead to the staff room. She looked towards the lake. She looked towards the main building. She started walking up the path.

She knew that the boy in her dream was Johnny. Even though she hadn't seen his face. Even though there was no good reason why Johnny should come slow-dancing into her unconscious thoughts. She walked towards the music and the lights. This is ridiculous, she told herself. You don't even like each other very much. Why should she dream about him? Soundlessly, she approached the staff room. Through the window she could see the kids dancing, part of the heat of the night. At the back of the room, Johnny and Penny, forehead to forehead, moved together as one. It was with some relief that she realized that Penny was fully dressed. And there was nothing keeping Baby apart from them now. No tracks. No waves. She could just walk right in and join them if she wanted.

But still she watched, her face close to the glass, as though watching a movie. Everything about these kids was different to her, to the people she went to school with, the kids whose lives were all mapped out for them. She couldn't dress like they did. She couldn't talk like they did. She couldn't fool around the way they did. She couldn't take the chances they took. Maybe they didn't have all the opportunities she had. The money and the breaks and the connections. Maybe at the end of the summer she would go to college and a bright future, and they would go back to dead-end jobs, to stuffy little apartments, to a world she couldn't even imagine. But they had something she didn't have. They had possibilities. They had the possibility to surprise. To be unpredictable. To take a wild chance. To just up and go. Go to some other state, or some other country. Do something incredibly brave or incredibly foolish. Frances Kellerman, on the other hand, would probably do what everybody really expected her to do. Go to college, marry a doctor or a lawyer or an engineer, have two children, spend her summers at a Catskill hotel. But at least one of those kids in there had the possibility of doing something no-one expected. Might know what it was like to feel really alive. She watched Johnny's hips move against Penny's. Their world wasn't hers. She turned away slowly and started back the way she had come. It was a world she didn't know how to enter.

The lamp on the bedside table snapped on the minute she stepped inside the door.

Robin popped up in bed like a punch-bag clown. 'Where have you been?'

'I went for a walk.'

'At two-thirty in the morning?'

Baby flopped across her mattress. 'I was hot, I couldn't sleep.'

'You were hot and you couldn't sleep, so you went for a walk by yourself at two-thirty in the morning?'

'Yes.'

Robin stared at her as though waiting for some further explanation.

'Stop looking at me, will you?'

'But that's not like you.'

'Well, big deal,' snapped Baby. 'So I did something unexpected for a change. Next thing you know I'll be doing something really crazy like eating snails or dying my hair black.' Suddenly she started kicking her sheet to the floor. 'I hate my sheets!' she screeched. 'I hate my sheets, and I hate this heat, and I hate how boring everything is.'

'Baby—'

'Oh, Robin,' wailed Baby, staring up at the ceiling. 'Don't you ever want to do anything . . . anything . . . I don't know . . . anything *wild*?'

'Wild?' echoed Robin. 'What are you talking about *wild*? You mean like rob a bank, or run off with a Hell's Angel or something like that?'

'Oh, I don't know. Just something . . . different. Something that isn't all nice and safe like everything else in our lives.' She put her arms over her eyes. 'I'm just so tired of being good all the time. Of being *nice*. I want to be *me*, but I don't even know who me is.'

'What's wrong with you?' asked Robin, real concern in her voice. 'Is this some sort of adolescent crisis?'

Baby rolled over so she was facing the wall. 'Nothing's wrong with me, I'm just hot, that's all. I don't know how you can sleep in this heat.'

Robin lay back on her pillow. 'I was dreaming of Danny,' she said, glancing over to the bureau where his face smiled at her from the cover of his LP record.

Baby's shoes hit the floor, thud, thud. 'Is that all you ever think about?' she groaned. 'Men?'

'No,' said Robin seriously. 'Sometimes I think about clothes, and sometimes I think about food.' She considered the question, for a second. 'But mostly I think about men.'

'Well, I'm sick of it.' Baby suddenly reached over and turned off the light. 'That's exactly what's wrong with this place. Someone's always pining away or getting her heart broken or wanting someone she can't have . . .'

Robin propped herself up on one elbow. 'Baby,' she said, gently, peering into the darkness, '*what* are you talking about?'

Baby rolled over on her side. 'Shut up, will you, Robin?' she said. 'Can't you see I'm trying to get some sleep?'

Eleven

The staff was calling it the kitchen of hell. Not only because it was insufferably hot, but because it was so chaotic that working in it had become a punishment in itself. Two of the busboys had collapsed with heatstroke, one of the cooks had run off with a waitress from the Sheldrake, and the head waiter had broken his arm water-skiing. Baby and the others were working double shifts, and still being yelled at by everyone. The guests, getting restless and irritable as the heat wave dragged on, complained about everything. The service wasn't fast enough. The drinks weren't cold enough. The food wasn't fresh enough.

'I don't think I can stand much more of this,' Sheila, one of the other waitresses said to Baby. 'It's like trying to please my mother.'

'It's worse than that,' sighed Baby. 'At least you can't be fired from being a daughter.'

To top everything off, the bakery order had been short, the fish delivery had never arrived at all, and Max, worried about Jack Benny, was getting under everybody's feet.

'Yeah, yeah, yeah,' the chef was saying as Max trundled behind him, giving him advice. 'I know, I know, I know.'

Max put his hands on his hips. Not that the chef, supervising the fruit salad, could actually see him. 'Are you listening to me?' Max wanted to know. 'Have you listened to one word I've said?'

The chef sailed by him, on his way to check on the soup *de jour*, or soup of the jaws as he insisted on calling it. 'Every word is engraved on my heart.'

'Look,' yelped Max, exasperated, 'we've got a crisis with this darn heat wave. People are going to start leaving again if we don't keep them happy.' He stepped back as a waiter walked past with a loaded tray, nearly colliding with a waiter hurrying behind him. 'I want to see everybody happy.' He pointed through a gaggle of busboys and waitresses, towards the door. 'Those people out there are not happy.'

'What do I look like?' asked the chef, diving into the refrigerator. 'Loretta Young?'

Max was in no mood for jokes. 'The Wyatts are sitting there, salivating for their blueberry pancakes, while you stand around being a wise guy.'

The chef gave him a gentle shove out of the way and started to make the mayonnaise.

Max's voice rose. 'And as for whoever it was spilled the maple syrup all over Jack and Elaine Gable . . .' He shook his fist in the air. 'I want them fired immediately.'

'Don't worry about it,' snapped Baby, suddenly materializing beside him. 'I quit.' She tore off her apron and stuffed it into his hands.

Max watched her storm out of the kitchen with a baffled expression on his face. 'Now, what's got into her? he asked the chef.

The chef pointed towards the door. 'Max,' he said, trying to keep his patience, 'either you put that apron on yourself or you get out of here now. I can't afford to lose any more staff.'

Of course, Baby thought to herself as she stalked across the grounds, trying to pull herself together, you leave one hell and you walk right into another. Coming towards her, a smile on his face as big as a city block, was Neil.

'Hey there, Baby!' he leered, stopping right in front of her. 'What's the good word?'

'Not now, Neil,' said Baby, trying to get around him.

Neil blocked her. 'What do you mean, "not now"? The sky is blue, the sun is shining, the day is young and so are we.' He nodded towards the woods. 'I know a secluded little lagoon where we could be alone.' He waggled his eyebrows. 'What say we play a little hookey, Baby?' He ran one hand down her arm. 'We could cool off . . . and then we could heat up again.'

Was this the story of her life, or what? The only person interested in sneaking off for swims with her was Neil Mumford, America's answer to the Black Plague. 'Not now, Neil,' she repeated, giving him a shove that knocked him off his feet. 'I'm not in the mood.'

She thumped off in the direction she'd been heading. What she was in the mood for was sitting some place dark and cool and not having anyone whinging because the salt wouldn't come out of the shaker or the tea was lukewarm. Somewhere where there was no one telling her what to do. She crossed to the left. What she was in the mood for was sitting in the cool and quiet of the dance studio. She checked her watch. It was still too early for lessons, but Johnny might be there by himself, getting ready. She was in the mood for sitting in air-conditioned splendor while dance music played softly and Johnny limbered up.

It wasn't just a woman's work that was never done, Johnny reflected sourly, his eyes straying to the clock on the wall. A dance instructor's work was never done either. It wasn't even nine o'clock in the morning, he hadn't had so much as a cup of coffee, and here he was trying to turn Evelyn Ginzburg into a lithesome dance partner. If she'd been a cow instead of a middle-aged woman with blonde-white hair and an eighteen-inch waist, she'd have had four left feet instead of just two.

'That's it,' he said in a voice as smooth as honey, 'just bend with me. You've got it now.'

Mrs Ginzburg tittered. One of the other things that Evelyn Ginzburg had was an extremely wealthy and powerful husband who was rarely around. 'You make it seem so easy, Johnny,' she said, holding on to him just a little bit more tightly, 'so natural . . .'

Baby, already into the hall before she heard their voices, stopped at the door.

'It *is* natural,' said Johnny, his voice heavy with charm. 'Completely natural. It's what your body wants to do if you just let it.' His smile didn't waver as her hand moved down his back.

Another of the things Evelyn Ginzburg had was a liking for handsome young men. 'I wish I'd met you when I was younger . . .' she said with a sigh. 'Think of all the years of dancing enjoyment I've missed.'

Baby screwed up her face. Welcome to the Ark, she told herself.

'My husband doesn't begin to know how to lead the way you do,' Mrs Ginzburg continued.

If Robin had been there, Baby would have pretended to barf. 'Puke,' she'd have said, 'can you believe this?' But Robin at this moment was back in the cabin sitting in three inches of water in the bath tub, writing to Danny. So, instead, she made another face.

'It's just instinct,' Johnny was saying. 'When a man takes a woman in his arms, what does he have to know?'

Mrs Ginzburg leaned her cheek against his. 'You know, Johnny,' she said slowly, 'I know this time of day is inconvenient for you, but I'd really love another private lesson. I feel there's so much you've got to teach me.'

Baby wanted to go. Even the kitchen would be better than this, but something held her glued to the spot.

Johnny spun them around unexpectedly, pulling them apart. 'It'd be my pleasure, Mrs Ginzburg—'

'Evelyn,' she corrected, moving closer again.

'Evelyn,' he said, trying to get back the beat. 'There is no inconvenient time for a lesson for you. Evelyn.' He moved his lips to her ear. 'Dip,' he whispered.

Smiling, Mrs Ginzburg dipped. 'You know, Johnny,' she said, meeting his eyes, 'there just might be something I could do for you.'

He held her gaze. 'And what would that be?'

'My husband's opening a new review at his hotel in Vegas this fall. He's coming up tonight to catch Jack Benny. Don't you think it would be clever of me to let him discover you?'

His lips brushed her hair. 'Spin,' he said softly. And in the same voice, 'Very clever.'

Very clever, mimed Baby. Very, very clever. That's it, she thought, turning on her heel. One more second of this and I will be sick.

'My last class is at five,' said Johnny, while, unbeknownst to him, Frances Kellerman fled across the lawn. 'I'll bring the kids together after that and he can see what we do.'

It had been a mistake going back to the room. Robin, having had her breakfast and her lunch, written her daily letter to Danny and lost three games of ping-pong, was reading a movie magazine.

Baby, stretched out on her bed with a wet hand towel over her face, listened while Robin explained the details of Bobby Darin's love life to her.

Baby pulled the cloth off her face. 'I just don't get it,' she said, her voice full of disgust. 'What could he possibly see in her?'

Robin looked over, surprised. 'Well, you have to admit, Baby, she is pretty cute. And even if she's not as sweet as she's made out to be—'

Baby flung the wet towel at Robin. 'Not Sandra Dee, you jerk. Mrs Ginzburg.'

Robin, still immersed in Bobby Darin's and Sandra Dee's first romantic date, was finding Baby hard to follow. 'Bobby Darin's after Mrs Ginzburg? Isn't she the one with the leopard-skin pedal pushers?'

'Robin, come back to earth, huh? I'm not talking about Bobby Darin. I'm talking about Johnny.'

'Oh, Johnny.' Robin turned back to her magazine. 'I should've known.'

'He'll ruin his life.'

'I thought it was him and Penny you were worried about.'

'Me? Worried about Johnny and Penny?' Baby sat up. 'I don't know what you're talking about, Robin. Johnny can dance on the beach with anyone he wants.'

A beach in the Catskills? Johnny and Penny went dancing on a beach in the mountains? Robin opened her mouth to say that now it was she who didn't know what Baby was talking about, but Baby didn't give her a chance.

'It's the way he throws himself at these rich women that I can't stand. It's disgusting.'

Robin turned the page. 'It's his job.'

'I mean, he's never going to get over the train track, is he, if he keeps playing that game. He's always going to be over there with Shelley Fabares and Penny. He's—' Baby stopped abruptly when she realized Robin was staring at her with a dumbstruck expression on her face.

'Baby,' said Robin, tentatively, cautiously, almost as though she were dealing with someone who might suddenly turn dangerous. 'Are you sure you're all right?'

'I'm fine, Robin. I'm just hot, that's all.' She flung herself from the bed, grabbed her shoes and was heading for the door before Robin could make a move to stop her.

'But where are you going?' Robin called, standing at the screen door as Baby strode off.

'I don't know. I just want to be by myself for awhile.'

Robin sighed. What was it that made her think that being by herself wasn't what Baby wanted at all?

* * *

'Johnny, Johnny,' Norman was begging, 'I'll do the same for you sometime.'

Johnny was sitting on the floor of the studio, taking a break between lessons. He held the can of soda to his forehead, closing his eyes.

'Really, Johnny, I swear I will.'

Johnny opened his eyes. 'I don't get it, Norm. You're gonna miss an opportunity to have Jack Benny locked in a car with you? This heat must of melted what passes for your brain.'

Norman blushed. 'It's love, Johnny,' he said, looking at his hands. 'It makes strong men weak. It makes weak men strong. It makes hungry young comedians pass up the chance of impressing Jack Benny.'

Johnny raised an eyebrow. 'Love? After nagging the boss man for days to let you pick up Jack Benny, you want me to do it instead because you're in love?'

Norman nodded. 'Yes.' And then, feeling that more of an explanation might be needed, added, 'I've never been in love before.'

Johnny laughed, but it was an affectionate laugh. What a guy, he thought, Norman really takes the cake. He's in love so he's going to make the ultimate sacrifice just for the chance of a date with Myrna Glass. 'You must be nuts,' he said. 'You wouldn't catch me puttin' myself out for some chick. I wouldn't give up lunch, let alone a chance like this.'

Norm made a silly Norm face. 'Yeah, I know, Johnny, but that's the difference between you and me. You're a tough man of the world, and I'm just a schmuck from Brooklyn.'

Johnny gave Norman a friendly slap on the

head. 'Look, I'd like to help you out, Norm, but I've got a gig here at six—'

'No problem, no problem, Johnny. Benny's train gets in at four-thirty. You know all the shortcuts. It's not going to take you more than an hour to get to the station and back.'

'Well—'

'Just don't let Mr K find out, all right? He'd never let me live it down.'

Johnny shrugged. 'I don't know. I'd have t'juggle a coupla lessons around and—'

But Norman was already hugging him. 'You're a saint, Johnny, a real saint.'

Johnny grinned. 'A saint? *Me*? You wanna tell Uncle Max that? He seems to think I'm on the other team.'

Norman looked thoughtful – or at least what passed as thoughtful for him. 'Well, maybe you're right. Maybe not a saint. Maybe you're more like an apprentice angel.'

'Hey, yeah, that's me,' laughed Johnny. 'Johnny Angel. That's still better than what Mr Kellerman calls me.'

'Which thing he calls you?' asked Norman. 'The Jersey gigolo or Johnny Rebel?'

Twelve

Baby, walking along the deserted road, kicking stones, was beginning to understand why people in books were always wanting to 'get away from it all' and live in remote cabins in the woods. She looked around her. Out here, surrounded by trees and mountains and busy animals and insects, things seemed different. It was peaceful. It was beautiful. Things made sense.

Back at Kellerman's, she felt as though her life was never going to amount to anything. Twenty years from now, she would be just like all the other middle-aged women with their dyed hair and their cottage cheese diets and their facials who took mambo lessons and slipped the instructor twenty-dollar bills. She was never going to be the person she dreamed of being. She was never going to change the world. She was never going to feel again the excitement, the strange anticipation she felt when she was around a certain young man. Twenty years from now, would she be taking dancing lessons from some handsome instructor, holding him too close, saying to him, 'I wish I had met you years ago . . .?' And there was nothing she could do about it. That was what Sweets' and Martine's situation had shown. In this world, you were stuck where you'd fallen. She'd fallen into the role of Frances Baby Kellerman, a nice girl who brushed her hair one hundred times before she went to sleep each night and who never let a day go by without taking her vitamins; and Frances Baby Kellerman she would always be.

She stopped to pick a wildflower by the side of the road, tucking it behind her ear. Out here, she felt more like her real self. The person she was deep inside. The person with all the hopes and dreams and needs. She could breathe easier. She could think better. Out here, she almost didn't care with whom Johnny Castle danced on tropical beaches. Almost.

She stepped off the road as she heard a car coming up behind her. The car was slowing down. Baby looked up at the sky. 'Oh, no,' she said under her breath, 'don't let it be him.' The car was coasting behind her. 'God,' muttered Baby, 'why are you doing this to me?'

The car was beside her. 'Hey, Baby!' called Johnny. 'It is you! What are y'doin' out here?'

She wasn't going to look at him. 'I'm taking a walk. What are you doing out here? Shouldn't you be giving some private lessons or something right now?' She kept moving, the car crawling along beside her.

Johnny laughed. 'Yeah, I should be. But Norm was supposed to pick up Jack Benny at the train station, only he couldn't make it in the end. So I'm goin'. I thought I'd come the back way, to save time. Lucky thing I did.'

She glanced his way. 'And why is it lucky?'

' 'Cause I ran into you.'

'If you don't get going it won't be lucky at all, you'll be late.'

'No sweat, we've got plenty of time. Hop in.'

The car stopped. Baby kept walking.

'Hey!' shouted Johnny, leaning out the window. 'Where are you goin'? Don't you want a ride?'

'No, thank you,' she called over her shoulder. 'I'd rather walk.'

'You're nuts. You can't walk all the way back from here in this heat.' The car door opened and slammed closed. He got into step beside her. 'For once in your life don't be so freakin' stubborn. Where are you going all by yourself up here?'

When she didn't see or talk to him, she thought about him. When she did see and talk to him, she always wound up shouting. 'Look, I told you,' she said angrily, 'I'm taking a walk. Why don't you just get back in the car and leave me alone?'

'Does your father know you're up here on your own?'

She wanted to hit him. She was a peaceful, gentle person. She believed in pacifism. She loathed violence of any kind. Martin Luther King and Gandhi were her idols. But three minutes with Johnny Castle and all she could think of was doing him some bodily harm. Kicking him. Punching him. Knocking that stupid grin off his face with a large stick. 'I'm a big girl, you know—'

'I know,' he said, in a voice he rarely used with her.

She pretended that she hadn't heard him. 'I don't need my father's permission to take a walk. And I don't need a ride with you.'

'The other big girls don't usually put up so much resistance when I offer them a ride.' He grabbed hold of her arm. 'Come on, Baby, stop foolin' around. You shouldn't be up here alone. It's miles back. What if something happens to you?

What if you get eaten by a bear or somethin'? I'd never forgive myself.'

'Please.' She shook him off. 'You're breaking my heart.'

'I'm gonna break your head in a minute. Come on, Baby. Your father finds out I left you up here he'll be on my case worse than ever.'

'Can't you understand English?' she screamed. 'Or is money the only language you understand?' The words were out of her mouth before she even knew she was going to say them.

The humor left his smile. Of all the women he had ever known, Frances Kellerman was definitely the most maddening. Most girls weren't all that hard to understand, once you got to know them a little. You could usually tell where you were with them, what they wanted, what they expected. But not Baby. Oh, no, she was never going to let anything be too easy. With Baby, nothing was ever what it seemed to be. At least he was beginning to know her well enough to know that when he thought they were talking about one thing she was, in fact, talking about something totally different. 'Now what are we talkin' about?' he asked.

'Nothing, Johnny.' She hadn't meant to say anything like that; what had gotten into her? Maybe Robin was right and she was losing her mind. She stared at the ground. It was incredible just how many pebbles there were along the side of the road. You never saw them, you never thought about them, you never wondered how they got there – but there they were.

'No, you've been stompin' around, avoiding me for days—'

'*Me*? I've been avoiding *you*?' She kicked several pebbles into the road. 'I'm not the one with all the private lessons.'

He was Sherlock Holmes with the first clue. 'Private lessons?'

She put her arms out as though she were dancing. It was true that she was losing her mind. She seemed to be incapable of stopping herself from behaving badly. 'When a man takes a woman in his arm, Evelyn . . .' she said in a deep voice, '. . . what's he gotta know? It's instinct, Evelyn . . . it's you . . . you and your rich—'

'OK, that's enough. What are you, the Mata Hari of Kellerman's? Don't you have enough t'do, you've gotta spy on people?'

'I wasn't spying, I—'

He pointed a finger at her. 'Just stay out of my business, OK? It's my business, not yours.' Suddenly, he spun her around and started marching her back the way she'd come. 'Just get in the car now. I'm gonna be late.'

She struggled in his grip. 'I don't want to get in the car. What are you stupid or something? *I do not*—'

He wrenched the door open. 'In. Get. I may not be a brain like you are, Miss Kellerman, but I know it's more than my job's worth to leave you up here on your own.' He slammed the door after her.

'I don't even like Jack Benny,' Baby grumbled as they screeched back onto the road.

'That's OK,' said Johnny, his eyes straight. 'If he's got any smarts he won't like you either.'

Max and Sweets were walking through the main building, doing one of Max's Walking Tours. Sweets called it his Cheerleader Routine.

Whenever something special was happening at Kellerman's, Max insisted on parading through the resort beforehand, reminding everyone of what was happening, making sure that enthusiasm was high.

'Hey, there, Mr Levy,' Max called as he and Sweets strode into the bar, 'I hope you have your best suit pressed for this evening. You're going to laugh more tonight than you've ever laughed before.'

'Really, Max,' Sweet mumbled under his breath, 'you should've been a social director.'

'Mr and Mrs Samuels!' beamed Max. 'Don't forget, even while you're sitting here sipping your spritzes and eating your peanuts, Jack Benny is at this moment heading this way.'

Sweets put a hand on his wrist. 'Oh no he's not,' he said softly.

'Dr Brown, Mrs Brown, I hope you remember that—' Max's smile died, his voice failed. He turned to Sweets. 'What are you talking about?'

'Didn't you say Norman was pickin' Benny up?'

'Uh huh.'

Sweets nodded across the room to where Norman, minus his Kellerman's jacket, was hurrying through the door, his eyes on his watch. 'Then who's that?'

'Norman!' shouted Max. 'Norman!'

Norman stared at him like a rabbit caught in the headlights. 'Mr Kellerman!'

Max strode over. 'Well, now we know who each other is,' he said, pushing Norman against the wall. 'Just where the heck is Jack Benny?'

'At the station?' guessed Norman.

'Well, that's one right answer,' said Max grimly. 'Shall we try for two, Norm? Why aren't *you* at the station?'

Norman swallowed hard. 'It's just . . . I had . . . something came up, Mr Kellerman. I just couldn't make it after all.'

Max stared at him in simple awe. 'You mean, something came up that was more important than Jack Benny? You mean, Jack Benny is at this moment walking twenty-five miles in ninety-degree temperatures because you had something better to do?'

Norman shook his head. 'No, no, Mr Kellerman. I wouldn't do a thing like that. It's all taken care of. Someone else is picking Jack Benny up.'

Max's color started to go back to normal. His breathing showed signs of stabilizing. 'Oh, thank God, thank God for that. Somebody else has gone for Benny.' He turned to Sweets with a weak smile. 'You, see, Sweets? There was no need to worry. Somebody else is getting Benny.' He brushed his fingermarks out of Norman's shirt. 'Who'd you send instead?'

Norman smiled triumphantly. 'Johnny.'

'Johnny?' Max repeated.

'Yeah, Johnny.'

'Johnny who?'

Norman looked nervously at Sweets. Sweets, about to laugh, turned away. 'Johnny Castle,' said Norman at last.

Max put his elbows on the bar and rested his head in his hands. 'Johnny Castle is picking up Jack Benny,' he groaned. 'Johnny, the king of the torn T-shirt brigade, is picking up Jack Benny.'

Sweets clapped him on the shoulder. 'Look on the bright side, Max,' he said encouragingly, winking at Norman.

Max lifted his head a full two inches. 'And what would that be?'

'Well, for one thing, Jack Benny's not a woman. So you know they're gonna turn up at some point.'

'Yeah,' agreed Norman. 'And for another thing, nothing worse could happen.'

The barman placed a phone on the bar. 'Call for you, Max.'

Max pulled himself together. 'Hello, this is Max Kellerman speaking.' His face lit up. 'Jack! Where are you? Don't tell me the kid didn't—'

Sweets and the barman exchanged a glance.

'Come on, you old kidder. I know you're not in New York. I had to turn people a—'

'What is it, Mr K?' whispered Norman, trying to put his ear next to the phone so he could hear.

Max slapped him away. 'OK, yeah, so someone dropped out of the telethon . . . well, of course you couldn't refuse, yeah, yeah . . . I'm waiting for the punchline, Jack, I— . . . Uh huh. Uh huh . . . Wait a minute, Jack, wait a minute . . . I've got guests who've come here just to see you . . . I've got a contract—' Max signaled to the barman for a drink. 'Yeah, yeah, next month – No, of course not, no problem, what could be the problem? Right, right, I'll talk to you next week . . .'

The bartender put a glass in front of him.

Max hung up the phone.

'Bad news?' asked Sweets.

Max smiled wanly. 'Only if you'd packed the hotel on the basis that Jack Benny was coming up for the weekend. Only if you had busloads of people coming over from other hotels just to see him. Only if you'd planned this as the biggest event of the summer.' He made a sound like an accordion losing air.

Norman touched his am. 'Well at least there's one good thing, Mr Kellerman. At least you don't have to worry about Johnny anymore.'

Max gazed into his drink. 'I always have to worry about Johnny,' he said softly. 'That's the one thing in this life I can rely on.'

The sky was still blue and the sun was still shining. But the car had stopped moving. It was now parked on the side of the road, overlooking an especially beautiful valley, its doors open, its hood up, its owner bent over the engine, cursing softly to himself.

'What's wrong with it?' Baby was standing behind him, peering over his shoulder. 'Do you know what's wrong?'

'Yeah, it won't go.'

'I don't believe this,' said Baby. 'How could this've happened? This sort of thing only happens in movies.'

He turned to her with a scowl, narrowly missing banging his head on the hood. 'Now you're talkin' to me again, right? For ten minutes you won't say a word, but now that we're stuck out here in the middle of freakin' nowhere, with Jack Benny turnin' into soup at the train station, waitin' for us, you want to talk. Just shut up, will ya?'

'Don't snap at me,' she snapped. 'It's not my fault the car stalled. I'm not the mechanic.'

He slapped a small part into her hand. 'No, but you will be, Miss Fix-it. Just stick with me.'

Thirteen

Night had fallen on the Catskills. It was a warn, still, moonlit night. The only star missing was Jack Benny. A peaceful night for the animals scurrying through the woods, and the couples dancing in the gazebo near the water – but not for Max. Since the fatal phone call, he'd been running around like a chicken with its head off, trying to arrange the entertainment so that Jack Benny wouldn't be missed. There was Johnny and Penny's special routine. Norman was ready with some new material – which meant that it would have been old for Jack Benny but was new for Norm. And a few of the guests had been signed up for an impromptu talent show, the prize a trip to Las Vegas to see Jack Benny at the Sands. All in all, not a bad bit of patch-work. It was with a sense of some relief that he started towards the dining room for his nightly check that everything was going smoothly and that his guests were all in a state of active pleasure.

'It's gonna be all right,' he congratulated himself, as he strolled along the verandah. 'Another disaster diverted by Max Kellerman, Super Businessman.'

And then he noticed Robin standing outside the dining room, looking out towards the distant mountains.

'Hey there, Robin,' said Max, leaning against the railing beside her. 'Where's Baby? She's not still mad about this morning is she?'

Robin looked at him blankly. 'Where is she?' she repeated.

A few hours ago, ruin licking him in the face, he would have lost his temper at her answer, but now he was his usual, easy-going self. 'Yes, Robin. Where is she? Still sulking in your room?'

Robin's eyes got shifty when she was tampering with the truth. They shifted now. 'Uh, not exactly, Uncle Max.'

A tiny bell of warning began tinkling in a corner of Max's brain. 'Well where exactly then? She go for a moonlight swim or something?' He laughed. What an idea, Baby going for a moonlight swim!

Robin nodded gratefully. 'Or something.'

'Or what?' persisted Max.

'Um, uh . . .' said Robin, not knowing where to look. 'She went for a walk.'

Max sighed with relief. For a second he'd been afraid that Baby, in one of her moods, had decided to go back to the city. 'Oh, right, she went for a walk. So where'd she go? Down by the lake?'

Robin's eyes darted from the tops of his shoes to his elbow to a point behind his head to the large pine tree that stood in front of the building.

'Robin,' he said, gently, kindly, patiently, 'just when did Baby go for this walk? A while ago? She isn't going to miss her supper, is she?'

Robin mumbled something he couldn't quite catch.

'What?'

'Before lunch.'

'*Before* lunch? Robin, it's after eight o'clock. What do you mean she went out before lunch?'

'I mean she went out before we had lunch,' said Robin unhappily.

'I thought you were meant to be keeping Baby company, Robin. I trust you to make sure she doesn't get in any trouble.

'I tried to stop her Uncle Max—'

For the second time in only a few hours, Max buried his head in his hands. 'Why me?' he moaned. 'Why does everything happen to me?'

'Now what?' asked a voice behind him. 'The dog die?'

Max turned around instantly. 'Oh, Sweets, thank God it's you.' He grimaced at Robin. 'My niece here has just seen fit to inform me that Baby went for a walk before lunch today and isn't back yet.'

Sweets waved aside his worry. 'She probably just walked too far, Max. Why don't you have someone go look for her?'

Immediately, Max looked happier. 'That's a brilliant idea. I'll send one of the boys.' He looked thoughtful for a second. He shook his head. 'It'll have to be Johnny, I guess. He doesn't go on for another hour and a half.' He gave Sweets a man-to-man look, lowering his voice as though he thought Robin wouldn't hear him. 'Of course, he's the one who knows these back roads the best.'

Sweets put an arm around Max's shoulder. 'Now, you're not going to get upset when I tell you what I'm about to tell you, are you, Max?'

Max looked at him warily. 'What?'

'Well, y'see, Max, I just came out lookin' for you because Penny's in a bit of a panic herself.'

There were times in life when you didn't want to hear what you knew you were going to hear.

And as far as Max was concerned, this was one of them. 'Penny?'

'Yeah, Penny. It seems that Johnny hasn't come back yet from not pickin' up Jack Benny.'

Robin caught her breath.

'It's after eight, Sweets. He left to pick up Benny before four.'

'I know. Penny' s worried he's had an accident.'

Max looked up at the sky. Max looked out across the grounds. The Catskills was a large mountain range. There were acres and acres of woods, miles and miles and miles of road. Somewhere out there, beneath those stars, was his youngest child, his precious Baby. And somewhere out there, beneath those stars, was Johnny Castle, the boy that God had invented just to drive Max Kellerman crazy. What were the chances that they were together? One chance in a hundred that they were? Or one chance in a hundred that they weren't? 'If he hasn't had an accident,' Max muttered under his breath, 'he will have when I get my hands on him.

Nature was one thing in the daytime, when the bats were sleeping, and most animals were shy enough to stay hidden, and you could see where you were going. But at night, no matter how many stars were scattered across the sky, it was something else. Every tiny sound was a mountain lion. Every yard seemed like a mile.

'I'm tired, Johnny. How much further do you think we have to go?' Baby was limping behind him, determinedly trying to keep up and not trip over anything. Nature isn't much fun either when the person you're walking through it with is mad at you.

'How the heck do I know?'

Baby managed to get in step beside him. 'I said I'm sorry, Johnny. What more can I say?'

'Nothin'.' He shook his head. 'Of all the stupid things t'do, losing that rotor.'

'It was an accident! I'm not the one who parked beside a ravine!'

'I didn't exactly park, Miss Kellerman. I more like ground to a halt. The least you could of done was hold on to what I told you to hold on to.'

'It was all greasy. It slipped!'

'Yeah, and the flashlight slipped too.'

'I thought I heard a bear.'

'You thought you heard a bear . . .'

'Yes, I did. I'm sorry if I'm not the mountain man you are. Next time I think I hear a bear I'll challenge him to a wrestling match.'

Johnny glanced over at her, hiding his smile. 'You just better pray nobody comes along and steals my car radio, that's all.'

'I'm surprised you didn't take it with you,' she snapped. 'Why you had to lug that stupid blanket—'

'Stupid? You think the blanket's stupid? I took it for you, Miss College Girl, in case it gets cold. It could get cold, you know. We're pretty high up.'

A bat skimmed overhead and she grabbed hold of him with a shriek. 'Oh my God, what was that?'

'Ooooh,' he started mussing up her hair. 'It was a vampire, Baby, it was after you . . .' He was laughing now.

She put her hands over her head. 'I don't see what's so funny.' She sounded nervous.

'Oh come on, Baby,' he said more kindly, 'you don't have t'worry. I'm here to protect you.' He put his arm around her in a friendly, big-brother way.

A shiver ran through her. Maybe Johnny'd been right about the blanket. Suddenly the night seemed chilly.

Baby cleared her throat, searching for her voice. 'Hey, what's that?' she asked, stepping away from him.

He grabbed her hand, laughing again. 'It's probably Big Foot.'

'No, look!' she pointed with the hand that wasn't being held by him. 'Isn't that a cabin?'

He squinted down the road. 'Yeah, that's a cabin all right. So what?'

'So we could sit down a minute.'

'Sure, why not?' he sighed. 'We've got nothin' t'hurry for now.'

'Ladies and gentlemen,' Max was saying, 'as you know, due to an unfortunate accident, Jack Benny is unable to be with us tonight.' There was a groan of sympathy from the audience. 'And I know that you will join me in wishing him a speedy recovery—' There was a burst of applause. Max held up his hands. 'But I'm sure that the show we've got lined up for you will be a fitting tribute to that great comedian . . .'

Penny, pacing up and down outside the entrance to the ballroom glanced in as Mr and Mrs Stein – The Great Magico and his Assistant – took the stage. She turned to Norm and Robin who were standing beside her. 'Oh my God, is this a nightmare or what?' she moaned. 'Johnny's out there, maybe hurt or somethin', and Mr and Mrs Stein are doin' magic tricks.'

'I'm sure Johnny's all right,' said Robin. 'I mean, he's a good driver—'

'Yeah,' agreed Norm hastily. 'You don't have to worry about Johnny. Probably something happened to the car.'

Penny shook her hands at him. 'Yeah? So? He's also a great mechanic. If somethin' happened to the car, he'd fix it.'

'If he could,' said Norman. 'But maybe something went wrong and he doesn't have the right part. Have you thought of that?'

Penny still looked worried, but a little of the fear had left her eyes. 'Yeah, well, I guess that coulda happened. If he was takin' one of his stupid shortcuts there's no tellin' where he's stuck.'

'You see,' said Robin, cheerily, 'there's nothing to worry about. It's Baby that's got me scared.'

Penny turned to her sharply. 'Baby? Why? Where's Baby?'

Robin took a step backwards. Unlike Johnny, who always made her feel like a real person, Penny always made her feel like a part of insect life. 'Well, uh . . . we don't know. She went for a walk this morning and she hasn't come back yet.' She smiled feebly.

Penny did not smile back. It was obvious that she was thinking hard. 'She went for a walk?'

Robin wasn't the only person Penny made feel like a beetle. Norman laughed nervously. 'Yeah, it's really crazy, Penny . . . I mean, you'll think this is really funny . . . but Mr Kellerman, Mr Kellerman thinks Baby and Johnny are somewhere together.' He laughed a little more heartily. 'Isn't that funny? Baby and Johnny together.'

'It's hysterical,' said Penny flatly. 'I think I'm gonna bust my garters.'

'I knew you'd think it was funny . . .' Norman trailed off lamely, looking desperately at Robin.

But Robin was staring in at the ballroom, where the audience was roaring with laughter. 'Hey, look at this,' she said brightly, desperate to change the subject. 'Look what Mr Stein is doing to Mrs Stein! He's pouring water all over her.'

'That's nothing,' said Penny grimly. 'Just watch what I do to Mr Castle if he misses our dance because he's out joy-riding with the little princess.'

'Here we go,' said Johnny. 'Candles!'

Baby stood at the door, looking around in the dark. Remote cabins weren't all they were cracked up to be. Even without the candles there was enough moonlight to be able to see that the cabin was filthy and starting to fall down. At the very least, there were bound to be spiders and mice. She wasn't particularly fond of spiders and mice. In some ways, she'd prefer to take her chances with the bears. 'I don't know, Johnny,' she said, trying not to sound as scared as she felt, 'this place is a little spooky. Maybe you're right and we should just keep going.'

He lit a candle, stuck it into an old bottle, and put it on the floor. 'Nah, you're right. We've been walkin' for hours. We need a rest.' He spread the blanket out on the floor and collapsed on it with a sigh. 'Come on, sit down.'

She hovered in the doorway. 'You don't think there are any bats in here, do you?'

'Baby, please. I've just messed up my chances of becoming a close personal friend of Jack Benny's. I've just messed up my chances of getting a gig in Vegas. I've just lost my job.' He peered at his watch. 'And at this very moment, no doubt,

Penny Lopez is stickin' pins into a wax image of me 'cause we're supposed t'do this new routine tonight and I'm not there, I'm here – and all you can worry about is bats.' He laid back on the blanket. 'Gimme a break, will ya?'

'Don't be silly.' She crossed the room and sat down gingerly. 'My father's not going to fire you after I tell him what happened. And Penny will forgive you.' She looked out the window at the distant stars. 'She always does, doesn't she?' she added in a whisper. 'And as for Mrs Ginzburg and her rich husband—'

'Baby, please, I'm not up t'one of your lectures tonight.'

'I'm not lecturing you,' she said, in exactly the tone she used for lecturing. 'I just don't understand why you think you have to throw yourself at these dreadful women just because they have mon—'

'Whoa, whoa.' He propped himself up on his elbows. 'You're a little mixed up here about who uses who. I don't throw myself at them, Baby, they throw themselves at me.'

'I'm not mixed up. I heard you—'

'Did I miss somethin', Baby? Did we get married or engaged or somethin' when I wasn't lookin'?'

She turned away from him. 'God forbid!'

'Well, good. Then I don't know how come any of this is your business.'

'It's not my business. It's just that I hate to see you waste your—'

'Look at me,' he ordered. 'I'm not gonna have this argument talkin' to the back of your head.'

She looked at him.

'That's better. Now, let's just establish one thing

here, okay? My job is to teach dancing. The more private lessons I book up, the happier your father is with me. If I started turning the Mrs Ginzburgs of this world away, I would be on my way back home before you could say "mambo". Can you understand that?'

'My father—'

'Your father calls me everything he can think of behind my back, but the simple truth is that he wouldn't keep me around if the ladies didn't like me.' He got up and went to stand by the window.

'Yeah but—'

'Yeah but nothin'.' He was so silent for a few minutes that she almost thought he'd fallen asleep. Then all at once he spoke, sounding farther away than the stars in the sky. 'Not that it's any of your business,' he said slowly, 'but all I do is teach dancin'. That's all. I smile and I flirt, but I know when t'keep my feet on the floor.'

Baby sat at the edge of the blanket, her arms around her knees, staring into the darkest corner of the room.

'You hear me, Baby?'

'Yes,' she said, her voice a whisper.

'You understand what I'm sayin'?'

'Yes,' she whispered again.

He wiped a heartful of dirt from the window pane. 'Good.'

When she spoke again her voice was stronger. 'It's funny, you know,' she said, 'but it's like once people start seeing you a certain way you can never get out of that. You're the bad boy, and I'm the good girl. Everybody thinks you're nothing but trouble, and that I'm nothing but sweetness and light. But it's not like that, is it? You're the ni—you're not really bad at all. And I . . .' Her voice shook slightly. 'I . . . I don't know, I'm just tired of everybody treating me like I'm this sweet little girl. There's another side to me, too.' When he didn't say anything she turned around. He was still looking out into the night. 'It's like we're trapped in these images people have of us. No matter what we do or what we're really like . . .'

'Yeah,' he said, 'I know what you mean.'

She rocked back and forth. 'Anyway . . .'

'Anyway,' he said suddenly, clapping his hands together and coming back to the blanket. It's past ten now. So what we've gotta decide is if we're gonna spend the night here or wait till the morning when we can actually see where we're goin'.'

'Spend the night here?'

'I know it's not the Waldorf, but I thought you were nervous about walkin' in the dark.'

'Well, yeah. Well, fine.' She scrunched over towards one side of the blanket. 'We'll spend the night here.'

Johnny lay down on the opposite edge. 'You're OK, right?' he asked over his shoulder.

Baby lay down on her edge. 'Yeah, I'm fine.'

He leaned over and blew out the candle. 'Right. Well, good night, Baby.'

'Good night. Sleep tight.'

'Yeah, you too.'

Fourteen

The talent show was proving so bad it was good. Max and Sweets stood offstage as the tenth star act of the evening, Sam and Charlie, the ventriloquist routine, performed to an enthusiastic audience.

Sweets, like just about everyone else, was laughing uproariously. 'It's hard to tell which is the dummy,' he grinned at Max.

Max was twitching. 'Look at the time, Sweets! Where could they be?'

'Max, man, I'm tryin' to enjoy the show. Will y'let it rest for a while? I'm tellin' you. If she's with Johnny, which I think she must be, then she's all right. Stop tying yourself in knots, will ya?'

Max jammed his hands into his pockets. 'He better not be ruining more than the dance number . . .'

'Max! Never mind trustin' Johnny. Don't you trust Baby?'

Max twitched. 'Of course I trust Baby.'

'Then what are you worryin' about?'

Max looked across the stage, to where Penny and her stand-in partner waited in the opposite wings. Penny, too, was twitching. And she also kept looking at her watch.

'I'm worried about what she's worried about,' said Max.

* * *

'Johnny?' called Baby softly. 'Johnny, are you asleep?'

He lay so still he almost seemed afraid to move. 'No,' he said at last.

'How come? Aren't you tired?'

'I thought I was, but all of a sudden I'm wide awake. What about you?'

She rolled over on her back. 'I was just lying here thinking.'

'Yeah, me too.' He hesitated for a moment, and then rolled onto his back, too. 'What were you thinking about?'

'I was thinking about what we were saying before. You know, about how people have these ideas about us . . .' She folded her arms across her chest. 'But at least, you know, it doesn't matter so much for you, because you know exactly who you are and what you want.'

They stared at the ceiling in silence for several minutes.

'Yeah, maybe,' he said at last. 'But I'll tell ya, somethin' I've never told anyone else. Sometimes I don't know what I'm fightin' against. Sometimes I think it would be a lot easier just to tell my old man I'm gonna take over the garage and leave it at that. What's the sense of knockin' yourself out all the time for nothin'?'

'But it's not for nothing. You've got a real talent.' Her voice became passionate. 'You're such a special per—' She caught herself. 'You've got such a special gift. But I don't. The only talent I ever had was an extraordinary ability at making Mr Potato Heads—'

Johnny looked over, smiling. 'I don't really know what I want,' Baby went on, not meeting his eyes. 'And when I do think I know, I don't know how to get it. It always seems just out of reach.' She took a deep breath. 'So what I do is I do what everybody expects of me, but I really don't know anything about myself.'

'Sure you do. You're Frances Kellerman, the girl who's gonna save the world.'

'Don't make fun of me.'

'I'm not makin' fun of you, Baby.' He propped himself on one arm. 'Look at me,' he said gently. 'I don't wanna say this to the side of your head.'

She turned so they were lying face to face, the moonlight spilling over them. It was almost as though she were dreaming, caught in a moment of magic – but she wasn't dreaming, the moment was real.

'That's better,' said Johnny. She could see in his eyes that he was affected by the moment and the moonlight too. He leaned towards her. 'I think maybe you have more of an idea of who you are than you think you do, that's all. I can feel it in you. I can hear it when you talk about your dreams and how you think the world should be.' He was silent for a few seconds, and when he spoke again she could hear the struggle in his voice. 'And I saw it, too,' he said, slowly. 'I saw it with Sweets and Martine—'

Her heart made an unnatural leap. 'With Sweets and Martine? But I thought—'

'Frances? Do you think you could let me finish what I was sayin'?'

'But you said—'

'I know what I said. And it's true, at first I thought you were totally off the wall sayin' they should go for it. I thought it was all just a loada pie-in-the-sky romantic crap. But then I started thinkin' about what you said. About how the world would never change if regular people didn't change their own lives. An' that if love doesn't matter then maybe nothin' does.'

Her heart had stopped jumping around, but was still beating fast. 'Yeah, but Johnny, in the end you were right. It didn't work. They couldn't make it.'

'Yeah . . . well . . . But that doesn't mean they shouldn't of made it. And it doesn't mean that . . . well, you know, that doesn't mean that some other couple won't make it. Maybe, for some reason, they just didn't want it hard enough.'

Baby gulped back an unexpected tear.

In the moonlight, Johnny reached out and touched her hand. 'You should stay true to what you believe, Frances Kellerman,' he whispered, 'no matter what anybody else tells you.' He gave a little laugh. 'Even me. It's like in dancing, y'know? You've gotta listen to the beat of your heart.'

'Yeah,' she answered after what seemed like a lifetime. 'I guess it is.'

'Yeah.' He brought his hand away. 'We better get some sleep, Baby.

'Uh huh,' she said, not taking her eyes from him.

'Right,' he said, not taking his eyes from her. 'Good night.'

'Good night.'

Slowly, they turned away. As slowly as the movement of the moon across the sky.

'So then the rabbi turns to the priest and he says, "And you shouldn't be here, either!" '

The audience burst into spontaneous applause. Robin and Penny, sitting together at a table towards the back, clapped too. If anybody had told Robin yesterday that she and Penny would be drinking Tabs together and laughing at Norman's jokes she would have told them they were crazy. And if anybody had told Penny yesterday that tonight she and Robin would be exchanging fashion advice and cheering each other up, she would have laughed in their face. And yet here they were, side by side like old friends. Isn't life strange, Robin thought to herself. Penny agreed with Chuck Berry: it goes to show you never can tell.

Robin looked over at Penny's tense, white face. 'You've got to stop worrying,' she said. 'Norm said if they're not back by the end of the show he'll go looking for them himself.'

Penny's long, red nails tapped on the table. 'Yeah, yeah, I know.'

Robin watched her silently while Norman told a joke about a cup of chicken noodle soup and a chihuahua. 'Are you afraid he's in a ditch, or are you afraid that he isn't?' she asked at last.

Penny laughed. 'Half and half.' She looked over to where Max was laughing louder than anybody else. 'It's the first time Mr Kellerman and I have had anything in common.'

'Baby?' whispered Johnny. 'Baby, are you asleep?'

'No,' she whispered back. 'Are you?'

He gave her a gentle kick, surprised to discover that she wasn't as far away from him as he'd thought. 'No. Every time I close my eyes I start thinking again.'

'Me too.' She sat up. 'You know what this is like?'

'You mean aside from one of the worst days of my life?'

She rested a hand on his shoulder. 'Yeah, aside from that.'

Here it was one of the hottest nights of the year, and her hand still felt warm. 'No,' he said, deciding that it might be better if he sat up too, 'what's it like?'

'It's like that song. You know, the Everly Brothers song.'

He laughed. 'You mean "Wake Up Little Susie"?'

'Yeah, that's the one.'

'If your father gets holda me before we get a chance to explain,' Johnny gasped, laughing even harder, 'it'll be more like "Dead Man's Curve".'

Baby collapsed against him. 'Oh my God, can you just picture his face?'

'Picture his face?' Somehow, her face was only inches away and looking right at his. 'Can you hear him? "You no good Jersey gigolo . . ." '

Baby wiped the tears from her eyes. 'H-how do you know he calls you that?'

Johnny grinned. 'You'd hafta be dead not to know what he calls me,' the smile on his lips fading as he got distracted by the look in her eyes. 'And I'm not dead.'

'No,' said Baby, 'you certainly aren't.'

'No,' he said, not sure whether she was moving towards him or he was moving towards her, 'neither are you . . .'

'No . . .' she said, lifting herself up to meet his lips . . .

Baby was back on that beach in the moonlight, the beach in her dream. Only this time she had crossed the tracks that separated her and Johnny. This time there was no Penny, there was no Shelley Fabares, there was no orchestra. This time there was only the two of them, and there was nothing between them, nothing keeping them apart, nothing—

It was Johnny who pulled away. 'Baby,' he said, trying to get a hold of himself, 'Baby, we can't . . . not like this . . .'

He was on his feet before she was even sure what was happening. 'Johnny, what's the matter?'

He reached for her hand. 'Call it delayed maturity or somethin', but we've got to stop this now.'

'But Johnny—'

He tugged her to her feet. 'Baby, we've gotta get outa here. This is wrong . . . you and me, like this . . . We can't spend the night alone here together . . . not now . . . I can't . . . we can't—'

She put her fingers to his lips. 'Johnny, shhh. It's OK, you're right.' She leaned her head against his chest, listening to his heartbeat. 'I understand.'

'Well, at least we showed Jack Benny,' Max was saying to Norman and Penny. 'I want to thank you two for helping to make this night such a roaring success.'

Neither Norman nor Penny could believe their ears. Max Kellerman thanking *them*? This was a turn-up for the books. But then, Penny thought, catching the smile Robin was giving her, this had been an odd night all around. You'd think there had been a blue moon or something.

Norman stood up. 'I guess I'd better hit the road, see if I can find Baby and Johnny.'

Robin grabbed her uncle's arm. 'Wait a minute!' she cried excitedly. 'Look over there by the side door!'

'Baby!'

'Johnny!'

'Thank God,' breathed Max, clambering to his feet. 'They're all right.'

Penny closed her eyes in a silent prayer. 'I knew he was all right,' she said when she opened them again. 'Didn't I tell ya, Robin? Didn't I say I knew they were all right?'

'Well, whatta y'think?' winked Johnny as they came through the door. 'You think your old man's gonna hit me first or hug you?'

'Oh, no, Castle,' laughed Baby, 'you've got it wrong. The question is: is Penny going to hit me first or hug you?'

He grinned. 'I guess there's only one way t'find out . . .'

'I guess so . . .'

Their smiles met.

'Hey, wait a minute, you've got some dirt on your face.' He reached into his pocket and pulled out a handkerchief. 'Here, use this.'

Baby wiped at her face, then looked at the small white cloth with the red 'F' in one corner that she held in her hand. 'Where'd you get this, Johnny? This is mine.'

'Is it? You musta lent it to me one time.' He snatched it back and jammed it into his jeans. 'Anyway, it's not yours anymore.'

As they crossed the floor Sweets started the band playing 'Blue Moon'. Baby stopped in her tracks. Just an instant there she'd been sure that what they were playing was 'Our Day Will Come'.